On the Volcano

On the Volcano

James Nelson

G. P. PUTNAM'S SONS

AN IMPRINT OF PENGUIN GROUP (USA) INC.

G. P. PUTNAM'S SONS

A division of Penguin Young Readers Group. Published by The Penguin Group.
Penguin Group (USA) Inc., 375 Hudson Street, New York, NY 10014, U.S.A.
Penguin Group (Canada), 90 Eglinton Avenue East, Suite 700, Toronto, Ontario M4P 2Y3, Canada
(a division of Pearson Penguin Canada Inc.).
Penguin Books Ltd, 80 Strand, London WC2R 0RL, England.
Penguin Ireland, 25 St. Stephen's Green, Dublin 2, Ireland (a division of Penguin Books Ltd.).
Penguin Group (Australia), 250 Camberwell Road, Camberwell,
Victoria 3124, Australia (a division of Pearson Australia Group Pty Ltd).
Penguin Books India Pvt Ltd, 11 Community Centre, Panchsheel Park, New Delhi—110 017, India.
Penguin Group (NZ), 67 Apollo Drive, Rosedale, North Shore 0632, New Zealand
(a division of Pearson New Zealand Ltd).
Penguin Books (South Africa) (Pty) Ltd, 24 Sturdee Avenue, Rosebank, Johannesburg 2196, South Africa.
Penguin Books Ltd, Registered Offices: 80 Strand, London WC2R 0RL, England.

Design by Ryan Thomann and Annie Ericsson.
Text set in Adobe Jenson Regular

Library of Congress Cataloging-in-Publication Data
Nelson, James, 1921– On the volcano / James Nelson. p. cm.
Summary: In the 1870s, sixteen-year-old Katie has grown up in a remote cabin on the edge
of a volcano with her father and their friend Lorraine, the only people she has ever seen,
but, after eagerly anticipating it for so long, her first trip into a town ultimately brings tragedy into
their lives. [1. Wilderness areas—Fiction. 2. Frontier and pioneer life—Fiction. 3. Violence—
Fiction. 4. Volcanoes—Fiction.] I. Title. PZ7.N43383Vo 2011 [Fic]—dc22 2008053557
ISBN 978-0-399-25282-2
1 3 5 7 9 10 8 6 4 2

For Jamie, Marie-Louise,
Jeffrey, and Rebecca

On the Volcano

Sometimes I dream I'm on the edge of our volcano, working my way through the brush, twisted pines, boulders, lava, and jagged rock, trying to make my way from our cabin to the other side.

The sun is blazing, I'm tired and thirsty, and I can't understand why I have no canteen. No canteen, no arrows, no bow, no dried berries, no beef jerky. How could I have set out this way?

I seem to be searching for someone.

Miles away, in the center of the crater floor, smoke belches from a hidden rupture.

I'm wearing an old pair of moccasins and the bottoms are thin. I feel every rock, every pebble. Last winter I made a new pair with thick, heavy soles. Perfect for an expedition like this.

Why didn't I wear them?

Who is it I am looking for? A boy, a girl, an old man? It doesn't matter. Just someone I can talk to.

I have so many questions.

The trail drops sharply. I slide, throw up a shower of rocks, fall in a heap. I lie there a minute, surprised, breathless.

I get up and trudge on.

As I go through a thick pine forest, branches whip at my face. I fend them off as best I can.

The forest opens. I can see a long way around the shattered rim of the volcano.

There's a person!

Walking away from me!

I shout, but no noise comes. I try to wave my heavy arms.

I try to run. My feet are stuck to the ground. I want to scream, but I can't get my breath, my breath, my breath.

At this point, I always wake up.

ONE

I rode into Badwater on a sorrel mare named Valerie, on the fifth day after my sixteenth birthday, disguised as a boy named George.

I rode out of Badwater three hours later, with a bloody cheek and a pounding headache.

I was no longer George. I was once again Katie MacDonald.

I was born out here in the Great Territories in 1855, in a lean-to high up on the edge of a crater overlooking a big, collapsed volcano.

My parents never planned to move here. They'd been living back in New Pacifica, in a town called Little Fish, on a river that led to the sea.

My father was a teacher and a carpenter. When he wasn't

teaching, he built houses and rented them out. He and my mother liked Little Fish and were very happy there.

But then some rebels tried to take over Salmonport, a town three hundred miles up the coast. They didn't succeed, but a few months later, they did manage to take over a town called Clark Harbor, just two hundred miles north of Little Fish. They had a lot more people this time, and better guns, and they held the town for over a week. Many people on both sides got killed, and it didn't end until the governor of New Pacifica called out two battalions of the Coastal Reserves, and the rebels were either captured or killed or driven out.

My mother and father didn't like that at all. Too many people had been killed, and the fighting was getting closer. They wondered if Little Fish might be next.

So, they decided it was time to move far, far away, out to the Great Territories. They wanted to find a place where they could live without the fear of sudden invasion, or even death.

Father sold his five houses, and he made sure he got paid in gold coins, not paper. He figured the fighting might spread throughout New Pacifica and beyond, and then paper money could become worthless.

It took them a month and a half to reach the border of the nearest Territory. They spent the next three months going deep into it, looking for the right place to settle.

Eventually, they came to our volcano. They'd heard about it not long after they'd started their journey. It was said to be huge and remote and constantly smoking, which scared a lot of people. But they'd also heard it was covered with trees and had lots of game, the kind of place where they could live peacefully and without fear, even if the rebellion in New Pacifica spread as far as the Territories.

They built their cabin on the west rim of the caldera. What's a caldera? It's the giant crater left after an enormous volcano has exploded and fallen back in on itself. Ours is twelve miles across. That's a *big* caldera.

I was born in the spring of their first year. It was hard living at first, but they both liked it, because they felt they were accomplishing something. But then, late in the second winter, my mother got sick with the fever. And before the winter was over, she died.

My father has a picture of my mother, and I ask him over and over what she was like. Her name was Sarah, and he loved her very much. He says she was very beautiful, and I can see that from the picture. She was a good rider, too, he says, and she could always make him laugh.

"She was an equal partner in everything we did," he told me. "She was the smartest person I ever met, very brave, and I knew I could always count on her, even when things got rough."

I often think about my mother when I'm out hunting birds or deer. As I scan the sky or watch a game trail, I wonder what it would be like if she were still alive.

I try to imagine having a mother around our cabin. I love my father with all my heart, but still sometimes I get an empty feeling. I think about how nice it would be if my mother and I were sitting out on the porch together, watching the smoke rise from the volcano, she with her arm around me and, even though I am grown up now, stroking my hair and saying little motherly things.

That would be nice.

But back to our Badwater trip.

One morning I was cleaning Billy's stall—Billy's our horse—when my father came down to the barn.

He smiled and said, "Good work, Katie-Bird." Then he took a harness off a hook and started back out.

I tried to sound casual. "By the way, Father, when are you going to Badwater?"

It was mid-autumn and I knew he would go before the snows.

"Week or two, I guess," he replied. "Why?"

He sounded just as casual as I did.

"I'm going with you this time," I said.

He looked surprised.

I don't know what made me so bold. Every other time I'd *asked* if I could go. This time I'd said: Ready or not, I'm coming!

Of course, I knew I wasn't going anywhere unless he said so.

"I can be a big help to you, Father," I pleaded. "I can carry things. I can manage Billy when you go into a store. I can help pack him for the trip back."

Father put on the serious look he always gets when I bring up Badwater. "It's a dangerous place, Katie," he said. "There are stragglers from the rebels and deserters from the Coastals down there, and they don't much care for each other. You don't want to get in between them!"

Naturally, I know he's only trying to take care of me. But if I can take care of myself hunting alone on the volcano, where we have bears and wolves and mountain lions, why shouldn't I get along just fine in Badwater?

"As I've told you, Katie-Bird," he continued, "I'll take you when you're older. That's a fact. I promise."

"I'm already older, Father. I'm sixteen."

He raised his eyebrows. "Really," he said.

"Well, fifteen and a half," I said. "That's almost sixteen."

My father leaned an arm over the side of the stall.

"I know what you're going to say," I cut him off. " 'Badwater's no place for a girl. Badwater's a rough and dangerous town.' Well, I'm ready for a rough and dangerous town. I really am, Father. And you yourself said it's getting safer."

"I did?"

"I want to see some *people*," I said.

"I don't blame you, Katie-Bird."

"I don't care who they are," I pleaded. "I just want to see them, old, young, someone my own age, maybe even a baby. Anyone."

My father stood there, looking thoughtful.

"Do you remember when I was a little girl, Father, and Old Dan came by our cabin, wearing white buckskins?"

"I remember."

"Do you realize that besides Old Dan, you and Lorraine are the only people I've seen in my whole life?"

My father paused for a long time. "Well, Katie," he said, "I'll have to think about it."

I had the feeling maybe I'd scored a point.

Father gathered up Billy's harness and walked back out into the sunshine.

Lorraine is a wonderful person who comes to stay with us from time to time. She was a nurse back in New Pacifica and now she travels around to remote cabins and homesteads to help people out. She's been doing it for years. When she comes to stay with us, she just appears, riding her horse Valerie. Lorraine helps with the chores, and she helps my father and me do jobs that are too big for two people. She may stay a long time or a short time, then she goes off again.

Lorraine is beautiful, especially when she smiles. She has sunburned skin and hair that hangs to her waist, like mine. Hers is a dark reddish color and very thick. Mine is thick, too, but much lighter, the color of the honey we sometimes get from hives in the trees. Lorraine wears her hair in a long braid, and every night and every morning she shakes her braid out and combs it.

"Let's be *women*!" she always says to me, so I comb my hair out, too.

Lorraine has a scar that runs from the bridge of her nose to the far side of her left cheek. She must have got it a long time ago, because now it's just a tiny white line, almost as sunburned as the rest of her face.

Once when Lorraine and I were sitting on the porch, I asked her how she got the scar.

She touched it as though she had forgotten it was there. "I ran into trouble when I was very young."

"Young like me?" I asked.

She put her hand on my arm and laughed. "Much older than you, Katie-Bird, but still young."

After I'd told my father I was going to Badwater with him, I finished cleaning Billy's stall and went back up to the cabin. Father and Lorraine were sitting out on the porch, on one of our oak benches.

I sat on the other bench and began to soak up some of the autumn sunshine. "What a day," I said.

"Gorgeous," Lorraine agreed.

My father turned to Lorraine. "Katie-Bird here wants to go to Badwater."

"Well, Jack," Lorraine said, "she's only been wanting to go since she was nine."

"Badwater was a pretty violent place when she was nine," he said. "Whenever I went there, I felt as though I was taking my life in my hands."

"Why'd you feel that way?" I asked.

"One trip I saw a man shoot another man dead, right in the middle of the street."

"Really?"

"Really. And afterward the shooter just sauntered away, cool as you please. But then another fellow came out of nowhere, and he shot the first man."

"Did he kill him?"

My father nodded. "Put four bullets in him. Turns out one was a rebel, one a Coastal deserter."

"You saw all that?" I gasped. "What did you do?"

"I just rode out of town nice and quiet as if I hadn't seen a thing," he said. "I had my supplies, and I was leading a pack-horse, so I just made myself scarce as fast as I could."

"You never told me about that, Jack," Lorraine said.

"It was a long time ago. But even just last year," he continued, "two men got into a fight inside the general store. They knocked over shelves and upset the cash box. Then one pulled a gun, and the other ran out the door and the second one took off after him. I don't know how it ended, but I felt sorry for the poor storekeeper."

"I wish I'd seen that!" I said.

"Things like that don't make me eager to take my little daughter down there," he said.

"Your *little* daughter! I'm not little!"

My father kept on talking as though I hadn't said anything. "To be fair, though," he said, "the situation could be getting a little better."

"How so?" Lorraine asked.

"Well, for one thing, they finally got themselves a sheriff. That should help. And just this past year ten or twelve new families moved in. They must have two hundred fifty people down there now. Helps them outnumber the misfits who started the place. Size sometimes has a civilizing effect."

Something big was hanging in the air. Was Father actually going to take me? I held my breath.

He turned to face me. "So, here it is, Katie-Bird. I can't keep you on top of this volcano forever, so as soon as you turn sixteen, I'll take you to Badwater."

My long campaign had paid off!

"Oh, thank you, Father!" I cried. A shiver of excitement ran through me. I raced over and put my arms around his neck. I wanted to jump up and down and laugh. This was what I had been waiting for. I love my father and Lorraine and living on the volcano and all, but now I was going to see some *different* people! Maybe a lot of them!

Then I felt a different kind of shiver. How would these new people feel about meeting *me*? After all, they were town people, and I was a mountain girl. Would they like me? When I met one, what on earth would I say? Would they talk like me? Would I know how to behave in a town?

All that swept in and out of my mind, and suddenly I was excited again. I began to wonder if I really had to wait for my birthday. Maybe there was some way to speed up the process.

"I know you want to protect me, Father. I appreciate that, and I know that's why you're not taking me till my birthday."

"You're welcome, Katie-Bird," he said.

I put my cheek against his cheek. "But should you happen to decide it's safe to go earlier . . ."

He looked up at me sideways and smiled. "Birthday, old friend," he insisted. "Not till spring. Six months."

TWO

Lorraine stayed with us all winter. I loved that. We went out on snowshoes many times to hunt game. She had taught me long ago how to crouch so I could keep my body warm while we were waiting near an animal trail. This year she taught me how to tie my right glove to my wrist so I could take it off even faster and be ready to let an arrow fly when an animal appeared.

Hunting is very important to us, because our major job is to keep ourselves supplied with food. It's the major job for everything that lives—birds, deer, flies, mosquitoes, everything. Without food, we'd all be dead.

My father makes a joke that he used to be a civilized man, living in a town where he could buy food in a store. Now he's a hunter-gatherer.

But he's a civilized hunter-gatherer, because he likes to

read. You might not think we have much to read, living on the edge of a volcano, but we do.

When my mother came out from New Pacifica, she brought more than a dozen books with her. Father says they are her special gift to me. We have both read them many times, and I love them all.

Another reason it's great to have Lorraine here is that we can talk about things that don't interest my father. Like clothing. One winter day Lorraine taught me how to make a deerskin skirt. Up till then I'd worn only trousers, like my father.

"After all," Lorraine said, smiling over her shoulder at my father, "we're not *men*!"

My first skirt came just below my knee. When I put it on, all that air on my legs felt funny. But after I wore it awhile, I began to like it. I felt a sense of freedom, and it was easier to move. And I knew that when summer came, the skirt would feel cooler and more comfortable than hot deerskin pants.

Lorraine had a deerskin skirt in her pack, and we both put them on before dinner. When Father came up from the barn, we sashayed around the big room with our hair flying and our skirts swinging. He just stood there, his hands on his hips, laughing. Finally he shook his head and asked, "Where did you two come from? A dance hall?"

"Yes," Lorraine said. "How do we look?"

"Very beautiful," he said, "and a bit deranged."

Later that evening, I asked Lorraine to tell me her opinion of Badwater.

"Badwater isn't really a town," she said. "There are no fancy houses. It's just a place where a bunch of people looking for a place to settle got tired and quit looking."

"You make it sound great."

Lorraine laughed.

"I think I'm going to like it," I said.

Just after the first snow fell, Lorraine said she wanted to teach me how to defend myself. "In case you're ever attacked," she said.

"Who would ever attack me? I never see anyone except you and Father."

"It's still a good thing to know." She turned to my father. "Right, Jack?"

"Right," he said.

"First, we need to clear some space," Lorraine said.

We moved the chairs and the table against the walls of the big room. Lorraine told me to get out all the blankets and fur rugs in the cabin. We spread them on the floor to make a mat.

"It won't hurt as much when we fall," she promised.

We were both wearing our deerskin pants, not our skirts. In winter all that air flying around your legs is no fun!

We took off our moccasins and stepped onto the blankets, facing each other.

"I'm going to pretend I'm you, Katie-Bird," Lorraine said, "and you're going to be the attacker."

"Okay."

"First we'd better do something about our hair," Lorraine said. "I'll braid yours, you braid mine. It'll save time."

As I was braiding her hair, I asked, "Where'd you get your earrings, Lorraine?"

Her earrings are perfect gold circles. You can't see where they begin or end.

"My mother gave them to me when I was twelve."

"How did you get them through your ears?"

"My mother made a hole with a needle," she said. "Then she put the ring through the hole and closed the ring."

I cringed. "That must have hurt."

"Not if you want them badly enough," Lorraine said.

I touched one of the rings and made it swing back and forth in her ear. "Does that hurt?"

She laughed. "Heavens, no."

"They're beautiful," I said.

"So are you, Katie-Bird."

When I'd finished braiding Lorraine's hair, she turned around and put on a menacing look.

"Now. Attack me," she said.

I'd almost forgotten what we were going to do. "What?"

"Hit me," she instructed. "Make fists. Try to knock me down. Try to take something away from me. Anything."

"I don't want to hit you, Lorraine."

"Don't worry, you won't hurt me. Now, hold your hands up like this. If I try to hit you, use them to block me."

I held my fists up and tried to hit her shoulder lightly. While my arm was moving toward her, Lorraine caught it and yanked. I flew past her and landed in a heap.

"You've got to swing harder and faster," she said. "And

you've got to try to fool me. Don't let me know when you're going to swing."

I tried to be crafty. I danced around her from side to side. When I swung, I swung hard.

Halfway through my swing I was flying through the air again. I was glad we had the blankets.

"How do you do that?" I asked.

"That's what I want to teach you," Lorraine answered. "I want you to learn how to turn an attack back against the person who makes it. When he makes his move, you want to make him move a lot farther than he'd planned."

She handed me a blunt stick. "This is a knife," she said. "Stab me."

I was very careful this time. I circled her slowly. I watched her eyes. When she looked away for a moment, I leapt and stabbed.

I was on the blankets in an instant.

"I want to learn that," I said.

Lorraine smiled and looked at my father. He smiled back, but he didn't say anything.

"Let's do it slowly," she said.

She walked me through the moves. I swung at her methodically, and she took my wrist and pulled it in the direction it was already going. As my body went past hers, she stuck her hip out and forced me off balance.

We did it four more times. Always the same.

"Get the idea, Katie?" she asked.

"I think so," I said.

"Let's switch parts," she said.

Lorraine became the attacker. As her fist neared me, I grabbed her wrist and pulled. I stuck my hip out as she went by.

We did it over and over. Then we sped it up a little. After a while we sped it up even more. We did it for nearly an hour.

"We'll do this every night, Katie-Bird," Lorraine said. "I'll teach you some other things, too. You can fight with your feet, if you know how. But that's for later. By the time the snow melts, you ought to be pretty good."

Lorraine got ready to leave early that spring, even before the snow had finished melting.

"I'll be back before your birthday," Lorraine said. "I want to see the two of you take off for Badwater."

I hated to see her go. I would miss hunting with her, and baking bread with her, and all the funny things she said when she and my father and I were playing card games.

We were all three standing outside in front of the porch. The sun was shining, and Valerie was all saddled and packed. Far out in the middle of the volcano a broad, steady ribbon of smoke rose, up and up and up, until it faded into nothingness.

I watched it rise. I wasn't thinking about Lorraine going away but about her coming back. Then I would go to Badwater and see some people at last.

I knew I'd probably see people my father's age, running a

store or something, but I really wanted to see some girls my own age. I wanted to see if they were anything like me. What would they look like? Would they be wearing buckskins? Would they be pretty?

I wondered what the boys would be like, too. I supposed they would look like smaller versions of Father. Would they talk to me? What would I say if I met one? I'd think of something.

Valerie snorted. She seemed happy to be wearing her saddle again, to be going somewhere after the long winter.

We said our farewells, and Lorraine put a foot in a stirrup and swung into the saddle.

"Take care of each other," she said. With that she turned Valerie around, waved, and rode off toward the volcano's north rim.

After Lorraine had gone, I asked my father if he thought Lorraine was beautiful.

"Very much so," he said. "What do you think?"

"Oh, yes," I said.

I wanted to ask my father what he thought about me in that direction. I couldn't, of course. What if he thought I was plain? Lorraine had said I was beautiful, but she was a woman. From my reading, women sometimes viewed these things differently from men.

I'd read about good-looking women in some of my books. Like Elizabeth Bennet in *Pride and Prejudice*. She was gorgeous, and Darcy was handsome, but that didn't seem to make any difference until just before the end. In *Vanity Fair*,

Becky Sharp's beauty seemed to give her a power over men, and even over other women. But beautiful women didn't always come to a happy end in my books.

I kept on practicing everything Lorraine had taught me. I did it down in the barn. I pretended I was facing an attacker, and I went through all the moves.

It wasn't the same, but it kept me thinking about whether I was getting any better, and about who on earth I might use it on.

THREE

Lorraine returned three days before my birthday. She rode up looking healthy and sunburned, straight in her saddle, smiling at us both. I didn't realize how much I'd missed her until I saw her.

"About time," Father said, grinning up at her.

She swung down out of her saddle, and I gave her a big hug. We helped her unload, and then I took Valerie down to the barn. She and Billy seemed happy to see each other. I unsaddled her, put her in the stall next to Billy's, and gave them both a good feed.

When I got back to the big room, there was a waxed paper sack of chocolate candy called fudge sitting in the middle of the big table.

"In celebration of your turning sixteen," Lorraine said with a smile.

We each ate a piece right away. I couldn't believe how good it tasted! I held each bite in my mouth as long as I could before swallowing. I wondered if Lorraine had gotten the fudge in Badwater, and then I wondered—when Father and I went to Badwater—whether I would get to taste a lot of other new things.

We saved the rest of the fudge for my birthday.

My birthday dinner was partridge. It was just like any other dinner except Lorraine gave us hats to wear, made from crinkly red stuff she called tissue paper. For a present she gave me a beautiful leather bag she'd made. I'd watched her work on it during the winter, never dreaming she was making it for me. It had beaver fur on the outside and soft deerskin inside.

My father gave me a statue of an eagle. He'd carved it with his hunting knife and painted it with colors he'd made from wildflowers. It was a real surprise, because I never saw him working on it at all.

After dinner, we ate the rest of the fudge.

So now I was officially sixteen. Old enough to go to Badwater.

We spent the next day getting ready for our trip. Lorraine insisted we take Valerie so we would each have a horse. My father pulled our packs and hauling equipment together while Lorraine prepared our camping and cooking gear. I gave both horses a good brushing and fed them well.

We tried not to take too much. We knew we'd be bringing

back lots of supplies, and even with two horses, they'd be so loaded we'd probably have to walk.

That night I was so excited I could hardly sleep. I kept wondering if maybe I would meet a girl my own age, and we could become friends. She would tell me what it was like to live in a big town like Badwater, and I would tell her what it was like to live high up on a volcano that smoked all the time.

The sun was warm when I walked out onto the porch after breakfast. Far out in the distance, the volcano's smoke rose in a line so straight it could have been drawn with a ruler.

I gave Billy and Valerie a little extra breakfast. Then I saddled them and brought them up to the front of the cabin. All our gear was laid out on the porch, and Father began packing the horses.

After he finished, he handed me an old leather jacket. "Here. Try this on."

This seemed strange, but he was in charge of the trip, so I put it on, right over my buckskin jacket and my braid. It was pretty big. Then he gave me an old leather hat with a big brim.

"This, too."

It was even stranger than the jacket.

I looked at Lorraine for a clue. She just stood there, not giving any hint, so I put the hat on, too.

Father cocked his head. "What do you think, Lorraine?"

"Hmm," she said.

"Until we get back, Katie-Bird," Father said, "you're going to be a boy. Do you mind? You're going to be my son George."

"I don't understand," I said.

"Well, I know you're tired of hearing me talk about how dangerous it is in Badwater," he said, "but that's the truth. And that makes me think that maybe it's just as well nobody knows I've got a young, pretty daughter."

Pretty. My father had said I was pretty. Right out loud. I liked that.

"It won't matter to most people," he said, "but there are some fairly wild young men—and some fairly wild older men, come to think of it—that I'd just as soon didn't know."

"How wild are the younger men?" I asked.

"Well, they don't seem to have anything to do, so they just hang out around town and get in the way."

"Come inside a minute, Katie," Lorraine said. "We'll be right back, Jack."

Lorraine took off the new coat and hat and laid them on a chair. "You need a couple of minor adjustments," she said.

She braided my hair up high in the back and pinned it on top of my head. I put the leather hat over it.

I took my jacket off and put the larger one back on.

I looked in the mirror. "I've never seen a boy, Lorraine, but I can't imagine they look much like this."

I was hoping she would agree, and would talk with my father, and get him to call this boy thing off.

Instead, she said, "You're too clean."

She went outside and came back with dirt on her hands.

She rubbed some on my forehead and one cheek and on both sides of my neck.

"Do I have to do this, Lorraine? This coat is way too big."

"Your father thinks you'll be safer this way," she explained.

"Do I look like a boy to you? Honestly?"

Lorraine squinted. "You need more dirt. Roll up your cuffs. The arms are too long anyhow."

I rolled them up, and she rubbed dirt on the back of my hands and wrists.

I looked in the mirror again. I still didn't think I looked like a boy, but I sure did look dirty.

"Let me switch the stuff out of my other jacket," I said.

I took out my gloves, my spare bowstring, my folding knife, my all-purpose cloth, some leather thongs.

Finally, my magnifying glass.

My magnifying glass is special. Like the books, it's a keepsake of my mother's that my father gave me a long time ago. It has a circular silver case with my mother's initials engraved on it—S. T.—her initials before she married my father. The lens swivels out of the case when you want to look at something. I carry it with me all the time in the side pocket of my deerskin jacket. To make sure I don't lose it, I've made a second little pocket inside the first, with a button to hold the glass in.

I use it to look at things that are very tiny or to take a splinter out of my hand, things like that. Also, when the sun is shining, I can make a fire with it.

Everything went into the big jacket, all in different pockets. I turned back to Lorraine.

She looked me over thoughtfully. Then we went outside. She turned to my father. "Meet George."

Father looked, raised his eyebrows, and said nothing.

So it was settled. I was a boy. This was going to take some getting used to.

I was going to ride Valerie, and my father was going to ride Billy. He'd strapped his old saddle scabbard on Valerie. This was a long leather sheath he'd used when he had a rifle. He also strapped a scabbard on Billy, one he'd made from deerskin and willow rods.

"Put your bow in it," he said, "and strap on your quiver. Makes them easy to carry and you can get at them in a hurry."

My bow was longer than the scabbard, of course, and stuck out. It looked odd at first, but it wasn't in my way or Valerie's, and Father was right, it certainly would be easy to grab. I strapped my quiver on beside it. It had sixteen arrows.

Lorraine was giving me a good-bye hug when my father said, "There's one other thing I want you to know before we set out, Katie."

I turned to face him.

"You know I'm not fond of handguns," he said, "but the fact is I own one now. Got it last trip from a man who was selling up his goods to raise money."

I was really surprised.

"I knew you and I'd be making this trip sooner or later," he continued. "I got to thinking I might be more comfortable if I had this inside my jacket."

He opened his coat and took a gun from a pocket up near

the left armhole. He swung the cylinder open so I could see the bullets. He pulled one bullet out and put it back in.

"That is how you load," he said. He closed the cylinder and put the gun back in his coat. "I feel strange carrying it, but I thought you should know."

With that, my father kissed Lorraine good-bye and mounted Billy. I gave her a great big hug and a kiss and got on Valerie.

I had waited and wished and hoped a long time for this, and now it was actually here! It was exciting to think I was finally going to see Badwater.

We set off north along the crater's rim to avoid the boulders and hardened lava along the south rim. We angled down the side of the volcano for half an hour, then turned south and kept going. We didn't talk. All you could hear was the saddle leather working and the sound of the horses' feet. From time to time I heard a blue jay or a magpie. The pines smelled fresh.

I had a sudden thought. This was the first time in my life I wouldn't be sleeping at home. In my own bed, in my own room. I love our cabin, but as we rode along, it was exciting to think that I wouldn't see it for a week. Everything I'd see from now on would be new!

After a couple of hours we came to a small stream. The horses dropped their heads to drink, and Father said, "When we get to town, Katie, it might be best if you not say anything unless you have to."

I could understand that. I wouldn't sound like a boy. "I won't."

"If you're forced to speak, if something comes up where you've got to talk, make your voice as low as you can."

"Like this?" I croaked.

He looked at me thoughtfully.

We made camp just before dark in a small, flat meadow on the side of the volcano. For the past hour we'd had glimpses of the plain below through breaks in the trees. I thought it would be completely flat, but it wasn't. It rose here and fell there and stretched out toward a purplish range of mountains in the west.

We hobbled the horses, laid out our bedrolls.

"We'll eat a cold dinner," Father said.

"Why don't we make a fire?" I asked.

"I don't want anyone thinking people might actually live up on our volcano," he said. "You know how every now and then I have to exchange some of our gold coins for their paper money. Well, I don't want anyone creeping up our mountain trying to sniff out where that gold comes from. That's why I always vary my route just enough so I don't make a path. So, to answer your question, even though I doubt there's anyone within fifty miles of us, I don't want to take a chance with a fire."

"You've really thought this out," I said.

Father smiled. "I probably overthink it."

"But what about the smoke from our cabin?" I said. "If someone got close, wouldn't they see that?"

"People expect smoke from the top of a volcano," he said. "They'd have to be pretty darn close to tell it came from us, not the volcano. Smoke coming this far away from the top, however, might be a different matter."

Later, as I lay in my bedroll, I thought about someone coming up the volcano to look for our gold. I knew the volcano didn't belong to us, but I still hated the idea of anyone else being there. It would be kind of scary to be out hunting and to meet another person, especially someone who had come to rob you!

I looked up at the sky and tried to find the constellations my father had taught me a long time ago. I found Cassiopeia's Chair and the Swan right away. I was going to look for some others, but that's all I remember till I woke up.

FOUR

The trees thinned out the next morning as we rode farther south. We were still going down, down, down, but you could see it was going to flatten out sooner or later.

About mid-morning we came to what my father called a dry wash. It was a gully in the shape of a letter V, and it ran down the side of the volcano, crossing our path.

"Dry as dust," Father said, "but watch out when it rains. Turns into a torrent. Farther down it broadens out, and finally peters out on the flat."

Billy picked his way carefully down our side of the wash, crossed the small, rocky bottom, and climbed up the other side. Valerie and I followed.

We crossed two smaller washes before noon. In the early afternoon we reached a feeble stream. I asked my father where it came from. He said there was a little spring in the hills off to the southeast.

Things were really different now. The ground had flattened out and had a parched look. There was sagebrush and cactus everywhere.

Even though the country was dry and empty, I liked how different it was from the volcano. At first it seemed barren, but when you took time to study the ground, you could see tracks of small animals and the holes they lived in. I wondered where they got enough water to exist. Horned lizards appeared, not very big. They looked strange, not like any animals I'd ever seen before. Some of them would stay completely still as the horses went by, others would shoot off so fast you could hardly see them.

After half an hour our feeble little stream turned into a feeble little pond. We stopped and watered the horses. We sat down nearby, ate lunch, and drank sparingly from our canteens.

When we remounted, Father said, "Well, Katie-Bird, we've ridden south far enough. Now we'll ride west for a day or so, and then we'll ride north into Badwater. I want them to think we live south of them, not east."

We kept on riding west until sundown, not finding any water at all.

We made camp in that dusky time just after the sun has gone down. We were two days' ride from the volcano, but it still looked huge. I wondered how far we'd have to ride before it looked like a little hill.

As I unrolled my bedroll, I thought about how much I loved sleeping under the sky. I'd even seen a meteor.

I decided when I got back home, I would sleep like this from time to time, out in front of the cabin, staring up at the stars.

The third day we rode west till the sun was directly overhead. Then we turned north.

I turned to my father. "Now we're headed for Badwater, right?"

"Absolutely. You think the Badwater folks are going to think we come from the south?" he asked.

"They'd better!"

Father laughed.

We sighted the town an hour before dark. It was still a long ways away. It looked like a jumble of tiny gray boxes. Dirty smoke hung in the sky above. I felt a surge of excitement run through my insides. Those tiny gray boxes were filled with people! More people than I'd ever dreamed of seeing!

"Well, now you've seen Badwater," Father said.

I stood and stared. "Is this what towns look like back in New Pacifica?"

My father laughed. "No, towns back there are a lot neater, a lot greener, a lot more inviting. Badwater's a pretty sorry excuse for a town."

We rode on until we came to three big rocks thrust up out of the earth at an angle. We climbed to the top of the biggest one and surveyed the landscape. To our right, the top of the volcano was shielded in dark, angry clouds.

"Probably raining up there," my father said.

In front of us the town was in the middle of a big saucer. The saucer was miles across, and we were standing on one edge, looking down the slope to its dusty bottom.

"We'll camp here," Father said, "and tonight we'll make a fire. We want to make sure they see us now, see the direction we're coming in from."

The next morning we saddled up while it was still dark. We rode silently, chewing on deer jerky and sipping water from our canteens. Even though the sun was hidden at first, the morning gradually got lighter, and I got a fairly good look at the town. It was no longer a jumble, but separate houses.

I thought the houses would be made of logs, like our cabin, but many of them had smooth board sides. Some were even painted. Some had a second level, like one house on top of another.

My stomach felt all quivery as we entered the town.

The street was dusty, with houses on both sides. I wondered where the people were. I decided they were all inside, peeking out at us.

A man stepped out of a house on our right.

My first new person! I couldn't take my eyes off him. He wore cloth trousers and a leather jacket with a belt around his middle. His trousers were black and his jacket was brown, not buckskin, and he wore a black hat.

I watched him as closely as I'd ever watched a bird or deer. I wondered what kind of person he was, good or bad. Did he have a wife? A daughter like me?

He picked at something on the front of his coat, then looked up at the sky. Finally he turned toward us.

He watched as we rode by. My father turned in his saddle and raised his hand, hello. At first the man did nothing. Then he raised his hand slightly and let it drift slowly back to his side.

We came to a corner where a side street joined the one we were riding on. There were three houses on this street, all very small. One looked as though it needed a lot of fixing.

A large black dog stood by a tree in front of the nearest house. I had never seen a dog, but I knew from books that lots of people had them, and I was sure that's what it was. It was fun to see one at last. I stared at it as though it were an elephant. I'd seen deer, elk, bears, antelope, cougars, and here I was staring in wonderment at a dog.

It had floppy ears and a tail that curved upward toward the sky. As we got nearer, I whistled at him. I hoped he might come closer. Instead, he raised his leg and urinated against a tree.

I felt vaguely let down. Then I realized how silly that was. What did I expect him to do, dance?

Down the next side street there was a woman walking with two men. One man looked like he needed a good meal. He was tall and skinny and dressed all in black. The other man was shorter, carrying his hat and mopping the top of his shiny, bald head with a handkerchief. His head looked like a giant egg. The woman wore a long red dress and had a red kerchief tied over her head.

They stared right at us. I raised my hand, hello. The woman smiled and waved back. Some people were friendly! I waved at her some more and smiled. The man with no hair stopped mopping his head and looked at me, but nobody else waved.

That was four people. Three men and the nice woman who had waved. And a dog. It was starting to be a great morning, and we'd only just got here.

On the right-hand side of the street, a woman in a long gray dress was coming out of a falling-down barn backward, pulling on a rope. A huge black-and-white animal lumbered out after her.

"Is that a cow?" I asked.

"That's a cow," Father answered.

"Do you think she's going to milk it?"

"Probably, but we can't stay to watch."

Farther on there were several buildings, all made from sawn lumber, and two log cabins. They all had hitching posts and walks in front, also made of sawn lumber.

"Boardwalks," my father said. He pointed to a two-story building on the left. "That's the feed store. We'll stop on the way out. No point loading the horses before we have to."

In the next block we stopped in front of another two-story building. The first floor had a door in the center, a window on either side, and a boardwalk in front.

My father got off Billy and dropped his reins loosely over the hitching post. He knew Billy wouldn't wander.

"I've got to get some nails and a whetstone and one or two other things," he said. "Won't take long."

"Can I come?" I wanted to see the inside of the building. Even more, I wanted to see a person up close.

Father came near and spoke softly. "Sorry, but I just don't want anyone asking questions about you." He stepped up onto the boardwalk, turned back toward me, and spoke in a much louder voice.

"You stay here, George," he said. "Keep an eye on the horses."

I'd forgotten all about George.

I sat up straight in my saddle. What else should I do? Deep voice, I remembered that much.

Two streets away, a man came out of a building. He looked very small. I hoped he would keep coming, but he turned and went out of sight.

A few minutes later another man came out of a house. He glanced at the sky, then started walking toward me.

Keep coming, I thought, keep coming.

He was shorter and stockier than my father or the other men I'd seen. He wore ordinary leather trousers and a buckskin jacket, and he was wearing spectacles! I'd read about spectacles in books. The little wires over his ears looked uncomfortable. I wondered if the world looked different through spectacles.

As he got closer, he glanced at me. His expression didn't

change. I smiled and lifted my hand, hello, and as he passed in front of me, he nodded slightly and raised his hand.

I looked around. I suddenly realized there wasn't a single tree in sight. There were buildings and cabins, but not one tree. I was amazed. Where I lived, there were trees in every direction, and bushes and rocks and jet-black lava. I guessed they made up for it by having lots and lots of people instead.

It was strange. I'd lived my whole life in a place where I saw the same one person every day—two if Lorraine was with us—and now I was surrounded by people, people, people. Two hundred and fifty of them, my father had said.

What if they all came outdoors at once? It would look like an anthill!

Father came out carrying a coarse cloth sack with his hardware items. He stuffed it into one of his saddlebags, took Billy's reins, and climbed back into the saddle.

"How are you doing?" he asked.

"I saw a man with spectacles," I said.

He laughed. "You're going to see lots of new things. Now, let's go get the flour and sugar and the rest of the food list." We started on down the main street.

Two men on horseback came out of a side street. They rode toward us, and when they got close, one man held his hand up. I didn't know whether he was saying hello or stop. It didn't seem like just hello. We stopped and waited for them to reach us.

One of the men was about the same age as my father. The other was much younger, but I was pretty sure he was older than I was. They both wore boots, buckskin pants, big hats, and leather belts full of bullets, with guns hanging from them.

Father sat up straight in his saddle. Without turning his head, he said quietly, "I'll do the talking."

As they pulled up beside us, I saw stars pinned to their shirts.

"Morning," the older man said. He sounded friendly, but businesslike.

"Morning," my father replied.

"You folks just get in?"

"Just now," Father said.

"Where you from?"

"About two days' ride south of here."

"What town?"

"Tenspike's the nearest town," my father answered. "If you can call it a town. We live a few hours west of there."

It was strange. I had been raised to think it was a bad thing to tell lies. But I knew why my father was lying. To keep people from finding out about our cabin, and our gold, and to protect me. I guessed this was one time it was all right to lie.

"Mind telling me your name?"

"Jack MacDonald."

The man nodded toward me. "How about you?"

"My son George," Father said. "It's his first trip to Badwater."

The man was quiet for a moment. I guess he was thinking.

"My name's Benson," he said. "I'm sheriff for about as far as you can see in any direction." He nodded toward the younger man. "This is Deputy Summerfield."

The deputy raised his hand. "Adam Summerfield."

Adam Summerfield was the first person I'd ever seen who was anywhere near my age. I liked his looks right away. He was slender, and the way he sat his horse he looked tall. Taller than me anyway. He had a straight nose and deep brown eyes with long lashes. I hoped he would smile, but he didn't.

"Pleased to meet you," my father said.

"Where'd you camp last night?" the sheriff asked.

I felt sure he knew already. We'd made a fire the whole town could see. I wondered if this was a test.

Father turned in his saddle and pointed. "Up near that first outcrop."

"Plan to be here long?"

"Just long enough to get supplies."

The sheriff looked up and down the street, then turned back to us.

"Sorry for the interrogation," he said, "but it's my job to know who's in town and why."

"Makes sense."

"I might just tell you about a couple of drifters we're looking for," the sheriff said. "One's dark-complexioned, rides a bay gelding, the other's small and rides a pinto. They're both bad news."

"Good of you to tell us, Sheriff Benson," my father said. "What are they wanted for, if you don't mind telling me?"

The sheriff looked at me as though he wasn't sure he wanted to talk about it in front of me. Then he turned to my father and said, "Murder, to start with. And a few other things."

Father raised his eyebrows. "Murder," he said. "We appreciate the warning. We'll keep a sharp eye out."

"Well," the sheriff said, making it sound like a really long
word, "welcome to Badwater. Hope you find what you need."

"Thanks, Sheriff," my father said.

Sheriff Benson nodded, then managed to work up a smile.
The deputy looked like he wanted to work one up, too, but he
didn't. Maybe he felt that after what the sheriff had told us,
he shouldn't smile, whether the sheriff did or not.

The sheriff raised his hand, signaling the meeting was
over. My father and I raised our hands in return. The sheriff
and his deputy turned their horses and trotted off. We headed
for the general store.

FIVE

I didn't much care for what the sheriff had told us. Murder is an ugly thing even to think about. I wondered what on earth could make one person kill another on purpose. Now we would have to be even more cautious than we'd been, and we'd been pretty cautious.

I started looking around me and realized all over again that I was in Badwater, and that I'd seen four people—no, six now, counting the sheriff and Deputy Summerfield—and my excitement returned.

The general store turned out to be a log cabin. It looked something like our cabin, only a lot bigger. It was one story high, with six windows facing the street. The boardwalk in front was sort of like our porch, because it had a roof. There were other one-story buildings strung out on either side of the store. The covered boardwalk ran the length of the block.

Father draped Billy's reins over the hitching post. He came up close to where I was sitting on Valerie. Even though there was nobody around, he spoke softly. "I've been thinking, George, even when you make your voice low, you don't really sound a whole lot like a boy. Not your fault, that's just the way it is. So it might be better if you pretended to be a mute."

"What's a mute?"

"A person who can't talk," he explained. "Some people just can't do it. They get born that way, or they have some accident or something."

"So how do I do it?"

"Well, if someone tries to talk to you, don't say anything. Just open your mouth and point into it, and shake your head. That means you can't talk. You can hear all right, but you can't talk."

He stuck his hand in his pocket and pulled out his list. "This'll take a while. You all right? If you see anything that looks like trouble, you come running into the store, but just jerk on my sleeve, don't say anything. I'll come right out."

He looked up as though he wanted me to say something, to make sure I understood.

I pointed to my mouth and shook my head. Then I nodded.

Father smiled and went into the store.

For a long time I didn't see any new people. I just sat there and thought about what I'd seen. I thought especially about Deputy Summerfield. I'd read about young men in some of my mother's books, and I'd always wondered what it would be like to meet one in real life. And now I had, and it'd made my insides feel funny.

In my mother's books the young men sometimes fell in love with young women, the same way, I supposed, my father had fallen in love with my mother. I wondered if my mother hadn't been able to stop thinking about my father, the same way I couldn't stop thinking about Adam Summerfield.

It was crazy. He was just a boy. And I hadn't even talked to him.

A team of horses came down the street pulling a wagon. I could see from Billy's eye he didn't much like the rattling noise, but he and Valerie both stayed put.

The wagon hadn't been gone long before I heard voices. I couldn't quite tell where they were coming from. The voices got louder, and two young men came around the corner of the store. They stopped on the boardwalk in front of me.

Were they men or were they boys? They were big enough to be men, I would guess about the same age as Adam Summerfield, but they didn't act like men. Neither one wore a hat. One was tall, a bit on the heavy side, with stringy brown hair. He wore a purple shirt and a big, oval belt buckle made of some silvery metal. The other was about my height, skinny, with bright orange hair. Bright, bright orange. I had no idea hair came that color.

They were sloppy and noisy. Neither one looked anything like Deputy Summerfield.

They were arguing about who was the best shot with a revolver.

"Your dad doesn't even own one!" the orange-haired one said.

"He got one last week," the tall one replied.

"Have you shot it yet?"

"Not yet."

The boy with the orange hair laughed. "He probably won't let you. Has he got bullets?"

"He's getting some this week," the tall one replied. "A man's coming through town with ammunition."

"Hell, that's just talk, Jess. That guy's been coming for over a month, but where is he?"

It took me a minute to realize that, all the time they were talking, the tall one, Jess, was looking straight at me.

He took a few steps toward me. "Who the hell are you?"

That startled me. I sat up straighter and raised my hand, hello.

He took a few steps closer. "I said, what's your name?"

I opened my mouth, pointed in with my finger, and shook my head.

"What the hell does that mean?"

I sat still, looking him in the eye. I felt very uncomfortable.

"Can't you talk?" he said.

I shook my head.

"You're a goddamn dummy!" he exclaimed. He turned to his friend. "We got a goddamn dummy here, Marvin! Can't talk a word."

The orange-haired boy ambled over and stood by Jess. He looked up at me and laughed. "You can make a noise. You can at least do that."

I shook my head.

"Go on, make a noise!" Marvin said.

I opened my mouth, pointed, shook my head.

The two boys looked at each other.

"I can make him talk," Jess said.

He ducked under the bar of the hitching post and stood between Billy and Valerie, really close, looking up at me. Valerie stamped her foot and neighed, but she didn't move.

Jess fingered the bow in my saddle scabbard. He turned to his friend. "Look at this, Marvin, he brought his little bow and arrows to protect himself."

He started to pull at the bow. I grabbed it. He stopped pulling and looked up at me. "What's the matter? Can't I have a look?"

I shook my head vigorously. I was scared. There were two of them and one of me, and one of them seemed to want to make trouble. I'd never faced a situation remotely like this.

The skinny boy called from the boardwalk, "I don't think he likes you, Jess."

Jess kept looking up at me. "Don't you like me?"

I didn't want to nod yes, and I didn't want to nod no. I raised my eyebrows and shrugged.

"You just want me to leave you alone, don't you," Jess said.

I didn't move.

"Just take your hand off the bow so I can look at it, and

then I'll put it back. I just want to take a look, and then I'll leave you alone."

I held on to the bow.

"Don't you believe me?"

I shook my head. We both gripped the bow.

"I know you can talk," he said. "And you know you can talk. So just say stop, please, Jess, and I'll stop. And then I won't even look at your bow. Just say it. Just say stop!"

My father had said to come jerk his sleeve if trouble appeared. Somehow, that didn't seem like a very realistic option now. I wished the front door of the store would open and my father would come walking out and see what was going on. Right now!

I considered shouting, but I didn't think he could hear. Besides, that would give the whole George thing away.

I yanked at the bow, but Jess wouldn't let go.

Then he seemed to change his mind. "Oh, the hell with it," he said.

He turned as though he were going to leave. Then he gave the bow a yank that pulled me out of the saddle. I lost my grip on the bow and landed in the dirt between Valerie and Billy.

I looked up. The tall one, Jess, was standing on the boardwalk laughing. He had my bow in his hands and was pretending to shoot arrows. He pretended to shoot one at Marvin, then at me.

I got up. Half of me was steaming mad, the other half was scared. I went under the hitching post and stood there, on the edge of the boardwalk. Jess held my bow out in front of me as a taunt. Jess looked even taller now that I was on the ground, not on Valerie. I looked at him awhile, and at the bow, and then I started to turn as though I was going back to Valerie. Instead, I spun around and ran head down straight at Jess as hard as I could. I rammed him right in the middle of his stomach.

We clattered down onto the boardwalk together, my face scraping the rough boards. I got up as fast as I could and stood over him, fists up, ready to fight. I felt my cheek with the back of my fist. It came away bloody.

Jess got up slowly. He left the bow on the boardwalk.

"You little bastard!" He sounded surprised. "You're going to get it!"

He raised his fists and began to circle me.

I turned as he circled, trying to guess when he was going to try to hit.

He kept circling, moving forward, back, forward, back. Suddenly he lunged and swung hard at my face.

I grabbed his arm, yanked him toward me, stuck out my hip. He bounced off me, hit the logs on the side of the store, and landed in a heap.

Thank you, Lorraine!

I kept an eye on him and on his skinny, orange-haired friend, too. I was no longer scared. I just wondered what was going to happen next.

His friend seemed to think this was all very funny. He bent over laughing, as though he couldn't control himself.

Jess got up slowly. His forehead was bleeding. He came

toward me slowly and stopped. He lowered his hands and gave a big sigh, as though the whole thing was over. Then he charged me the same way I'd charged him.

He hit me in the middle, and I slammed onto the boardwalk on my back, with him on top of me.

"You're going to pay!" he hissed.

He got up on his hands and knees, legs astride me, his arms pinning mine down. He was breathing hard.

He let go of my arms and grabbed my head, hat and all, with both hands. He banged it hard on the boardwalk. "How do you like that?"

The blow stunned me, but at least my arms were free. I grabbed his wrists, tried to stop him, tried to make him let go.

He banged my head a second time. I saw bright lights, felt dizzy, but I didn't stop struggling. The third time he banged my head, my hat came off. The braid Lorraine had fastened to my head came loose.

"Hey!" Marvin exclaimed. "It's a girl!"

Jess stopped banging my head. He pinned my arms again and looked down at my face, at my loose braid.

"What the hell is this?" he said.

Lorraine had taught me a secret about kicking men. My head was spinning wildly, but I managed to work one leg loose. I thrust my knee upward as hard as I could and hit him, just where Lorraine said.

Jess screamed and rolled over onto his side, his legs pulled up toward his chest.

I stood up unsteadily. I picked up my hat. I put it on, just as a new wave of dizziness made me grab the hitching post to stay standing.

The store door opened. My father came out, carrying a gunnysack full of food.

He looked at me, braid dangling, cheek bleeding, hanging on to the hitching post.

His face turned dark. He dropped the bag and grabbed Marvin by the front of his coat. He stared down at Jess, writhing on the boardwalk, then at me. "Are you all right, Katie?"

"I think so," I said. I had never seen Father so angry.

He turned to Marvin, who was wriggling to get loose from his grip. "Did you touch her?"

Marvin shook his head. He looked scared to death.

"I said, did you do this!" Father shouted.

"No, no, I didn't," he said.

Father turned to me. "Did he?"

I shook my head.

He turned his head toward Jess. "How about him?" He nudged him with his toe. "What did you do to her?"

Jess shook his head and clutched himself a little tighter.

My father nudged him again, harder.

"I asked you a question!"

"Didn't touch her," Jess mumbled.

Father looked at me. "Is he telling the truth?"

"We had a fight," I said.

He nodded at Marvin, whimpering in his hands. "Did this one have anything to do with it?"

"No," I said.

Father jerked Marvin's coat together and brought the boy's face close to his own.

"Don't you ever let me see you again." His voice was low and menacing. "And don't even *think* of coming close to my daughter. Ever in your life. You hear?"

The boy shook his head up and down rapidly.

Father let go of his coat. The skinny boy ran up the boardwalk, turned the corner, and went out of sight.

My father turned his attention to Jess. "Get up!"

Jess groaned and shook his head. "Can't," he mumbled.

Keeping one eye on Jess, my father came over and looked at my face.

"You're the one who needs attention," he said. He put his arm around me. "Are you okay?"

"A little dizzy."

"Better sit down."

He led me to the edge of the boardwalk. I was a mess—head spinning, cheek bloody. I stuffed my braid under the hat.

Father got his canteen and knelt beside me. He moistened a cloth from his pocket and wiped my cheek very gently. He cleaned all the dirt from my face.

The cool water felt good.

He stood up and looked at Jess again. "Who did that to him?" he asked.

I didn't answer. My father looked around, as though there might be a third person he'd missed.

He turned back toward me. "You?"

I nodded.

He laughed. He looked at Jess, then back at me. "You did that?"

"Lorraine taught me," I said.

"You had a great teacher."

Jess was beginning to move. He eyed my father and began to scrunch away.

Father took three steps and stood over Jess, one leg on either side of his body. Jess stopped moving. "What's your name?"

"Jess," he answered.

"What's your last name?"

"Starkey."

"How old are you?"

"Seventeen."

"Seventeen," my father repeated. "Well, Jess Starkey, do you want to live to see your eighteenth birthday?"

Jess looked up at my father, not understanding.

Father bent over to get his face closer to Jess's. "Do you want to live to see your eighteenth birthday? It's a simple question."

Jess nodded.

"Then don't you ever look at my daughter again. Not even look. Do you hear me?"

"I hear you," Jess said.

"Louder!" Father insisted.

"I hear you," Jess said, louder.

"And if you ever see us riding down this street again," he said, "do you know what you'd better do?"

Jess shook his head.

"You'd better run and hide. Run and hide. You got that, Jess Starkey?"

Jess's head went up and down.

"Say it! What are you going to do if you ever see either of us again?"

"Run and hide," Jess said.

Father glared at Jess a long moment, then turned to me. "Think you can ride, Katie-Bird?"

I nodded and got up shakily.

He got my bow, strapped the food bag behind Billy's saddle, and mounted. I climbed onto Valerie and felt dizzy all over again. I hung on to my saddle horn.

We turned our horses into the street and started back the direction we'd come.

"I shouldn't have let that happen, Katie," my father said. "I'm very, very sorry."

"I'm okay, Father," I said.

"I just didn't want anyone to know you're a girl."

"But that's what I am."

My father leaned out of his saddle and put his arm around my shoulders. He held it there for almost a minute as we rode along side by side. I could almost feel his strength passing into my body.

"And thank God for that," he said. "You are a wonderful young woman. I wouldn't have it any other way."

I began to feel not quite so dizzy.

"We'll pick up our feed and get out of town. Sooner the better."

Father wasn't in the feed store long. I knew he didn't want to leave me, but he didn't want to take me inside, either, because he didn't want anyone asking questions. He didn't get as much feed as usual so we could get away fast. He wanted us to be able to ride most of the way and not have to walk and lead the horses. He didn't say so, but maybe he was also thinking about the people the sheriff had mentioned. He rigged one feed sack on each horse, and we mounted and headed out of town.

We hadn't ridden far before we saw two riders coming toward us. Father squinted, then whistled under his breath. "The sheriff."

"Should I be a mute?"

He didn't answer.

When we got closer, the sheriff held up his hand. Hello and stop. My father held his hand up in response. "Sheriff Benson," he said in a cheerful voice.

"Mr. MacDonald," the sheriff said. "And George. Well. Get everything you wanted?"

Father didn't answer. He looked at me, then back at the sheriff. "Sheriff," he said, "I want to introduce my daughter, Katie. Katie, this is Sheriff Benson, and if I'm not mistaken, Deputy Summerfield."

"Adam Summerfield," the deputy said.

"Hello," I said.

The sheriff didn't seem surprised I was a girl. He touched the brim of his hat and said hello, and Deputy Summerfield touched his hat, too. I looked them both in the eye, first the sheriff, then Deputy Summerfield.

For a moment I thought the deputy blushed.

"I thought this was George," the sheriff said.

"That was my idea," Father said. "I thought it might be safer here in town for her to be a George instead of a Katie."

"And how'd it work out?" the sheriff asked.

"Not too well," Father answered.

The sheriff turned to me. "What happened to your cheek?"

"I fell down on the boardwalk," I said.

The sheriff pulled his horse closer to mine. "You mind taking off your hat so I can see the full extent of the damage?"

I took off my hat and my braid tumbled down my back. I turned my cheek toward the sheriff.

"It's not much," I said.

The sheriff leaned out from his saddle and looked at me. Then he sat back, looking thoughtful. He turned to my father. "So now I guess you're heading back to Tenspike."

"Then west," Father said.

The sheriff lifted his reins, ready to ride. Deputy Summerfield did the same. He looked very handsome sitting there, motionless, erect. I got that funny feeling in my insides again. Our eyes met and held for a moment. I smiled. For a moment I thought he was going to keep on being serious, but after a few seconds he smiled back. A nice smile. I felt another shiver.

"Nice to meet you, Katie," the sheriff said. "Safe journey."

He touched his hat and Adam Summerfield touched his, and as they rode off toward Badwater, Adam turned in his saddle and waved. I waved back, and I almost thought I could see him smile again.

Father and I started off.

After about ten minutes Father said, "That sheriff wasn't born yesterday."

"What do you mean?"

"He knows we're not going to Tenspike, or anywhere near it."

"He does?"

"He doesn't know where we're going," he said, "but he knows for sure it's not Tenspike."

"How does he know that?" I asked.

"Because he's a shrewd man, and I'm a rotten liar."

We didn't say much as we rode up to the three rocks where we'd made camp on the way in. I don't know what was going through my father's head, but I started thinking about what had happened in front of the general store. Why had that boy Jess been so mean?

I'd done nothing to him. I was just sitting there, minding my own business.

What made a person behave like that? Suppose he'd known I was a girl to begin with, would he have acted any differently? Would he still have bothered me? Or would he have behaved even worse?

Everyone I'd ever known was kind and loving. Of course, I'd known only three people. Now I knew there were people who were mean and angry, people who went around picking fights.

Well, I thought wryly, I'd wanted to come to Badwater so I could see some people. Today I got my wish. I'd seen people, all right, but some of them I didn't care for very much.

But then there was the sheriff. He seemed like a nice person.

And there was Deputy Adam Summerfield. I knew for sure he was a nice person. You couldn't look like that, and sit your horse like that, and smile like that, and not be an extremely nice person.

Every now and then as we rode on, Father stopped and looked back. He scanned our trail, starting from the far left and moving very slowly to the far right, to see if anyone was following. Then he turned and scanned ahead, from one side to the other. With the sun under dark clouds, it was hard to see very far.

"I wish I'd brought my scope," he said.

We kept riding till way after dark. When we made camp, we both knew we wouldn't be making a fire.

SIX

The clouds stayed with us the next two days. The weather was warm, but it was moist, too, which my father said was very strange for sagebrush country. We kept up our lookout for anyone following us and for the two drifters.

On the third day we ate lunch and watered the horses at the same tiny pond we'd passed going toward Badwater. We were just getting back in our saddles when we heard thunder. Big, booming thunder.

It was hard to tell which direction it was coming from, because we couldn't see any lightning. We turned our heads one way, then another, listening.

"I think it's coming from the volcano," I said.

Father nodded. "It's raining up there," he said. "We'll have to look out for the washes."

I didn't say anything. Naturally, I wanted us to cross the

washes safely. But I also wanted to see what a torrent of water looked like when it came raging down.

We reached the first wash in about an hour. We'd already started climbing the edges of the volcano, but we hadn't gone very far.

"What do you know?" my father said. "Dry as dust."

He looked uphill, where the wash curved down toward us from a stand of trees.

"What are you looking for?" I asked.

"I'm not looking," he said. "I'm listening."

"What for?"

"When a wash starts running, all that water plus the brush and trees it picks up can make quite a racket," he said. "Even so, sometimes people don't hear a thing. That's why we look first, then listen, and if we don't see or hear anything, we cross as fast as we can."

"I don't hear anything," I said.

"Me either," Father said. "Let's go. You first. Hurry!"

"Come on, Valerie!" I said. I headed her down into the wash, sitting forward on the saddle, urging her with my feet and my voice. She went quickly but carefully, and in less than a minute we were up the other side. Father and Billy followed.

I looked up the hillside. If the wash wanted to send its flood down now, we were in a safe place to watch.

"Come on, Katie-Bird," Father said. "We've got two more of these things to cross."

The thunder returned overhead, louder, more threatening. The clouds were blacker than ever.

Father frowned. "There's a lot of action up there."

The second wash turned out to be as dry as the first. We looked, listened carefully, then crossed quickly.

Even before we got to the big one, we knew it was not like the first two. First we could hear the noise, and when we got there, a huge rush of water was roaring down the hillside, tumbling, grinding along bank to bank, full of brush and debris.

For a while we just sat there staring, leaning on our saddle horns. A small tree lumbered past, twisting and thrashing in the turbulence.

"A real gully washer," Father said.

It was hard to take our eyes away.

"Well," he said finally, "this is as far as we're going today. Might as well pick a camp spot." He nodded upward toward a little knoll. "How about up there? Dry. Safe. Great view of the goings-on."

I woke several times during the night. It was too dark to see the water, but each time the roaring seemed less.

For a while I lay awake and thought about Jess. I'd figured out the word for him. He was a bully. What made a person become a bully? Why would you pick on someone you didn't even know?

The next time I woke, the sun was coming up and my father was standing down near the wash, studying it. The flow looked almost peaceful. The water was still muddy but looked only two or three feet deep.

I joined him. "Is it safe to cross?"

He put his arm around my shoulders. "Maybe in an hour or so. Let's get some breakfast and pack up."

An hour and a half later the water had gone down another foot.

"A couple of feet aren't going to give the horses any problem," Father said. "I don't hear anything, so let's give it a try."

We saddled and packed and mounted.

"I'll go first," Father said. "You wait till I give the signal."

We approached the edge of the wash and stared down into it. It looked tranquil enough, even though it still carried some brush and an occasional small branch.

The horses didn't like it. They shuffled their feet and made movements as though they wanted to go back.

"Well, here goes," Father said. "Come on, Billy, let's go."

They slanted down the near side of the wash, and Billy's feet went into the muddy water. It turned out to be about a foot deeper than we had thought. Billy neighed a small protest as my father urged him across.

They were not quite to the middle when I heard it.

Looking up the draw, I saw the headwaters of a second gully washer. There must have been another cloudburst during the early-morning hours, and the water was just now reaching us. Roiling, churning, full of debris, it thundered down the wash.

"Father!" I shouted.

But he'd heard it, too, and now he could see it coming. He urged Billy forward in every way he could. Billy needed no urging. He and Valerie had heard the water long before

Father and I had heard a sound. No wonder they'd been so nervous.

Billy ran, scrambled, dodged, did everything he could, but it was all in vain. The muddy headwaters hit him broadside. The water knocked him off his feet and sent my father out of the saddle. Instantly they were both just another part of the flood.

I turned Valerie downstream, kicked her sides, shouted, "Go! Go!"

She responded instantly, moving as fast as she could, making her way along the irregular bank of the wash. Billy was out in the middle with his head pointed upstream. He was trying to swim against the roiling waters, trying to regain his footing. I couldn't see my father.

Valerie and I kept going and passed Billy. I looked and looked for my father's head.

Suddenly I saw him bobbing up and down, and somehow he was still wearing his hat. He was struggling to make it to my side of the wash but having no success.

And there was Billy, white-eyed, scared to death, trying to keep his head above water.

I rode farther downstream to get ahead of them. The wash got a little wider, the water a little shallower, but it was still moving swiftly.

I couldn't wait forever, so I slid off Valerie and untied the rope holding the feed sack. It fell with a big plop. I ran to the edge of the wash, tied a big loop in one end of the rope—my father had taught me how to tie a bowline—and got ready.

I coiled the rope, ready to make my throw. It had to be perfect. It had to reach him!

Here they came, Father and Billy. Billy was being dragged along on his side in the still-turbulent water, his pack weighing him down.

I waded out into the shallows, being careful I didn't get caught in the current.

Father was farther out than I'd hoped. He saw me. I swung the rope around my head and threw.

The rope fell short. Father sailed on by, half upright, fighting to find footing.

I hauled the rope in, got back on Valerie, and raced farther ahead.

The water had lost some of its speed.

Here came Father again. He was closer to my side now and trying to stand up, but the water kept knocking him back down. I waded into the shallows again and swung the rope out over the water.

He caught it!

He put the loop over his head and under his arms. I moved back onto the dry bank and dug my heels into the sandy soil. I felt the pull and dug in deeper.

At the end of the rope, Father swung in an arc toward the bank, stumbling, falling, but never letting go.

Closer, closer. He reached the bank, he was there! He climbed the side, soaking wet. I ran toward him.

"Great work, Katie-Bird!" he said, turning back to the wash.

Where was Billy?

There! Stuck on his side, across the wash, fighting to keep his head above water.

"I'm going out," Father said. "I've got to unload him or he'll never get up."

With the rope still around him, he climbed back down the bank and started across the wash. I kept some tension on the rope so he could lean against it and keep his balance as he picked his way through the water. When he reached Billy, he knelt beside him and held his head above the water. He put his head near Billy's ear. I couldn't hear, but I knew he was reassuring him, gentling him.

Still holding Billy's head in his arm, he reached for the cinch of the saddle with his other hand. He tugged and pulled and the saddle sagged from Billy's back. It disappeared underwater.

My father was still holding the cinch. He fastened the rope to it and gave me a signal to pull.

The saddle bumped along through the water. I got it to the bank and pulled it out.

Father was signaling for the rope again.

I picked it up, swung, threw, missed. I gathered it in, threw it, missed again.

I threw it again, aiming upstream from him. The rope half floated, half sank, but he finally got it.

He got the packs off Billy and tied them to the rope. I hauled them in.

When everything was off Billy except his bridle, Father

began to work him back and forth. He pushed on his shoulders, his legs, his back, trying to give him the idea that if he wanted to get up, he could.

Billy got the idea fast. He struggled, lurched, kicked his legs, tried to break suction with the mud. And then he was up, standing, looking dazed, and my father was leading him through the swiftly moving water toward the bank.

I watched them in brilliant sunshine. It was hard to realize that somewhere above us, not very long ago, there had been a fierce rainstorm. And here we were, dealing with its results in the warmth of a perfect day.

We spent the next two hours at the edge of the wash, cleaning Billy up. I made many trips down the bank, filling my hat with muddy water and carrying it back up to sluice Billy off.

When we were finished, we cleaned the saddle and packing gear. The feed sack was soaked, but we decided to take it along anyway. We would see what we could do with it when we got home.

After that, we rode back upstream. I retrieved my own feed sack, tied it on with the wet rope, and we continued our ride in the hot sun.

It was just past noon when we made camp on the same knoll as the night before. Father's clothes and bedroll were wet, so we squeezed out as much water as we could, then laid them out on the grass and let the sun go to work. We spread out my bedroll and the dry tarps from Valerie's pack and covered both of them with a layer of grain from the wet feed sack.

As the grain dried, we replaced it with more wet grain, and by nightfall, it was all dry. Father's clothes, however, his bedroll, and a number of other things were still wet. So we built ourselves a big fire, strung ropes between the trees, and hung the wet items as close to the fire as possible.

I had a sudden thought. "Father, what about the fire? Won't it be seen?"

"Lightning struck the volcano," Father said. "Caused a fire. Happens all the time during thunderstorms." He saw my doubtful face. "No, I don't like it either, Katie, but I did think about it, and lightning does start fires, and I don't think there's anyone close enough to come check."

I gave my father a blanket from my bedding roll, and we both slept near the fire. Once or twice during the night my father got up and heaped on more wood, to make sure everything got dry.

I was tired and went to sleep almost immediately. After about an hour, I woke with a start, shaking uncontrollably. I had been dreaming about the flooded wash, and I'd looked and looked for my father, but I couldn't find him. I'd ridden for miles up and down the sides of the wash, but he just wasn't there.

I sat up, shaking, tears streaming down my cheeks, and thought what it would be like if the dream had been true. Father was everything to me, my guide, my teacher, my protector, the person who loved me more than anyone else in the world.

Father's blanket moved. "Something wrong, Katie-Bird?"

When I heard his voice, my shaking began to taper off. "Bad dream," I said.

"Have you been crying?" He came over and knelt beside me. He put his arms around my shoulders.

"Nightmares can be terrible," he said. "I get them, too, now and then, and I hate them. But they're only dreams. Where we are now, this is real. You and me and the fire, and the horses."

He held me for a long time without saying anything. Then he kissed my forehead. "Think you can get back to sleep? No more nightmare?"

"I think so," I said. "Thanks, Father. I feel better now."

I didn't wake till morning. The fire was mostly out, and my father's clothes were dry and stiff, his bedroll as well.

From our knoll we could see that the wash was now full of puddles, but no water was running. We saddled and packed.

"You go first this morning, Katie," Father said, "but not till you hear me shout. I'm going to ride up this side of the wash to make sure there's nothing headed down. Not that I think it rained up there last night, but I want to make sure you don't get trapped crossing. When I shout, you go fast."

I waited until I heard his shout. Then Valerie and I scrambled down one side of the wash, across the bottom, and back up the other as fast as we could.

As I rode upstream on my side of the wash, Father came down on his side.

"I'll shout for you," I called.

"Thanks," he said. "I'm going to have to lead Billy across. He doesn't even want to look at it."

When we camped that night, we had the happy knowledge we'd be home the next day.

Lying in our bedrolls, I asked Father if he thought the volcano would ever explode again.

"I don't think so," he said. "It exploded once, don't you think that ought to be enough? But you can never be sure. What do you think?"

"Well, sometimes it makes those big, booming noises," I said. "Something pretty big must be going on down there."

My father nodded.

"Do you remember the night we saw lava spouting?" I asked.

"Yes, I remember. Very clearly," he said. "Putting on a little show for us."

I stared up at the inky sky, hoping for a shooting star, and thought about the volcano. I'd known it all my life. It didn't scare me.

SEVEN

Lorraine ran out to meet us. "Welcome back," she said. "I missed you both."

Father leaned down from his saddle and kissed her. She smiled up at him. "You smell like a campfire," she said.

She came over to me. I leaned over, too, and gave her a kiss.

"You too," she said.

Lorraine looked from me to my father. "You both look pretty bedraggled. What happened?"

My father laughed. "Katie got a few knocks."

"Looks like you hurt your cheek," Lorraine said.

"And I got caught in a wash," Father said. "Me and Billy. But Katie pulled us out."

"I just threw you a rope," I said.

"Well, that's what it took," Father said. "The right rope at the right time."

Lorraine looked concerned. "I want to hear what happened."

"Let's unload, and then we'll tell you about our adventures," he said.

My father patted Billy on the neck, and I patted Valerie. They'd both done fine jobs.

We unloaded everything except the feed bags. Then I took both horses down to the barn, unloaded the feed, unsaddled them, and gave them a rub. When I was through, I made sure they each got plenty of oats.

My father and Lorraine were sitting at the big table when I got back to the cabin. "Tell Lorraine about your fight, Katie," Father said.

"A fight?" Lorraine asked.

I laughed. "I'll tell you soon as I get out of these clothes, Lorraine. I can't wait to wear something that actually fits."

Back in my room I put the too-large George hat on a chair and the too-large George jacket on my bed. Then I put on my own dear buckskin jacket that fit me and that I loved more than ever after wearing the George jacket the whole trip. I began moving things from the George pockets into the pockets of my own jacket.

I moved my gloves. I hadn't used them. My folding knife, my extra bowstring, the leather thongs, my all-purpose cloth. I hadn't needed any of them.

I felt around for my magnifying glass. It wasn't in the left inside pocket where I'd put it. Or thought I'd put it, anyhow. And it wasn't in the right. Nor in any other pocket.

I searched each pocket again. Carefully.

Where could it be?

I ran out into the big room. "I've lost my magnifying glass!"

They knew what that glass meant to me.

"How could I have lost it?" I said. "It was in my left inside pocket. Now it's gone!"

Lorraine went into my bedroom and brought the George jacket back out into the big room.

"Could you have put it into your pack?" Father asked.

"I always carry it in my special button pocket," I told him, "but the George jacket doesn't have one."

He looked thoughtful. "I wonder," he said.

"What?" I asked.

"That fight," he said. "You got knocked down onto the boardwalk, didn't you? I wonder if it could have fallen out."

I thought back to the fight. I'd gone down twice, first between Valerie and Billy, then on the boardwalk, with Jess on top of me. I'd struggled, twisted, fought as fiercely as I could.

The glass could certainly have slipped out.

Then I thought about the wash. Could the glass have come out there? I'd been jumping on and off Valerie, running up and down the bank. But I'd been upright all the time. On the boardwalk I'd been flat on my back twice.

And then suddenly I knew, knew, knew that was where I'd lost it.

I felt hot tears run down my cheeks.

My mother's magnifying glass, gone!

I don't remember what comforting words my father and Lorraine said. I couldn't hear them. After a while I went back into my own room and threw myself on my bed and wept.

I had lost a piece of my mother.

By dinnertime I still felt sad, but I tried hard to convince myself it didn't matter. Of course, it did matter. It mattered a lot, but there wasn't anything I could do about it. It was too bad, it was a shame, but it was gone. Gone, I told myself, gone. Moping around wasn't going to help anyone, least of all me.

So, the three of us sat down together happily—well, as happily as I could, since all the stern talk I'd given myself hadn't really worked.

We had fresh venison. Lorraine had brought the deer down the day before with a single arrow. She'd put half of it aside in the cool house to eat fresh. The rest we'd make into jerky.

Over dinner we told Lorraine everything that had happened in Badwater. Meeting the sheriff. His warning about the two outlaws. About the fight with Jess. About the sheriff not believing for a minute I was a boy.

"Well," Lorraine said, "nice try."

I wanted to tell Lorraine about Deputy Sheriff Adam Summerfield. I wanted to tell her how brown his eyes were, about his long lashes, about how he'd smiled and waved. About how it made me feel just to look at him. But it seemed silly. There was no reason for me to be even thinking about him.

We told her the story of the dry wash. About poor Billy, and about Father, who despite being swept along through the turbulence never lost his hat, about drying things with the fire.

As I was finishing the story, my father started laughing. Lorraine asked him why.

"I was just thinking," he said, "about when I was a proper young man, living back in Little Fish. I never dreamed one day I'd be living out in 'those wild Great Territories,' as everyone called them, lying to a sheriff, looking out for murderers, riding down the side of a volcano on the headwaters of a flood, and here's the biggest part of the joke—thinking it was all just part of the day's work!"

Finally we got around to asking Lorraine how things had gone for her while we were on our journey.

"I had an exciting time, too," she said. "I had some sunshine and then I had some rain, a lot of rain, and then I had some more sunshine. Oh, and I finished a pair of moccasins. How's that for exciting?"

The sun was still in the sky when we finished our dinner. My father went down to the barn to clean up the tools and fittings he'd rescued from the wash. Lorraine and I sat on the porch. I'd missed seeing the crater. Smoke rippled out of the volcano in a wavy line that grew straighter the higher it got.

"I have another birthday present for you, Katie," Lorraine said. "I thought it would be better to give it to you when you got back."

"You already gave me the beaver bag," I said.

"I know," she said, "but these are different." She took a little box out of her jacket pocket and opened it.

I looked inside. There were two little rings.

"They're for you, Katie-Bird, if you want them."

"Of course I want them! Oh, thank you, Lorraine!"

"I hoped you'd like them."

"But I don't have holes in my ears," I said.

"I'll do for you what my mother did for me," Lorraine said.

We went into the big room and Lorraine stirred the fire. She put some water on to boil, dropped in the rings and a needle. Then she said, "Let me look at your ears. I want to make sure I put them in the exact right spots."

After the water had boiled awhile, Lorraine poured it off. I sat on a chair, and Lorraine pulled the hair back from my left ear. Very gently, she put a little pine chip behind my earlobe. Then she picked up the needle.

"Ready?" she said.

"Ready," I said.

I tried not to jump when she pushed the needle through my ear into the chip.

"Does it hurt?" Lorraine asked.

Of course it hurt, but I said, "Not if you want them badly enough."

Lorraine laughed. "Now I'll put the ring in."

I sat as still as I could. It didn't take long.

"There," she said, taking her hands away from my ear.

"Can I look?"

"Not yet. You have two ears."

The second ear took longer. Lorraine wanted to make sure she made the hole exactly even with the first. This one hurt, too, but I was too excited to care.

Finally, she was finished. She washed both my ears in cool water.

"Now you can look," she said.

I ran to the cracked mirror. I pulled my hair back on both sides and stared. My earlobes were pinker than usual, but right in the middle of each one was a round, gold ring. Just looking at myself, Katie MacDonald, wearing my new earrings, I felt a wave of excitement. Then I thought about Adam. It didn't make sense, but I wondered what he'd think. It would be a long time before Father would let me go back to Badwater, and I might not even see him if I was there. But if I *did* see Adam again, I imagined he'd like them.

I turned my head to the left, then to the right. I couldn't stop looking. "They're just like yours," I said.

Lorraine smiled at me, watching. I hugged her and buried my face in her hair.

"Thank you, Lorraine," I said. "I'm glad they're like yours, because I decided a long time ago I want to be just like you."

Lorraine took my hands and held them in hers. "You'll be a much better person than I'll ever be, Katie."

I ran down to the barn to show Father. He was looking at

one of Billy's hooves. I stood in front of him and pulled the hair back from my ears.

"Notice anything different?" I asked.

He looked at one ear, then the other. He smiled. "They add to your natural beauty," he said.

I gave him a hug and ran back up to the cabin.

EIGHT

During the late spring and into the early summer I did most of my hunting in the woods south of us. The hunting was unusually easy there, with plenty of doves and partridges.

But hardly any pheasants. We hadn't had pheasants in a long time, and once I thought about them, they sounded really good.

After chores one day, I said, "You know what? I'm going to that aspen meadow up north of The Crease and see if I can get some pheasants for dinner."

"Good luck," Lorraine said.

"Be careful," Father said.

I liked hunting pheasants. My father had taught me how to find them. It takes time and patience and thinking. They're not easy to shoot with a bow and arrow, either. They aren't small, but you can't get very close to them, and sometimes you have to shoot them just as they're taking off.

Father and I make special arrows to shoot birds. They have slightly lighter shafts and special tips that are less damaging than the ones we use for deer.

I got my bow and my quiver of arrows, half with the special tips, half with regular tips. I took a leather bag to carry birds and a small shoulder pack with a canteen and some deer jerky.

Father was on the porch, splicing a pack rope, when I left. No matter how many times I have gone hunting alone, he always says the same thing.

"Try to be invisible. Watch out for surprises."

"I will, Father."

"Hunt as though you're the one being hunted," he said.

From indoors Lorraine called out, "Enjoy yourself."

I started walking north along the crater edge and then turned downward to follow a path my father and I use a lot. After a while it peters out, and at that point you make your own path, depending on whether you're after birds or deer, or berries, or what.

I walked for about an hour, being careful not to kick stones or snap twigs, listening all the time. Before long I came to The Crease.

The Crease is a long, very deep slit in the ground about five feet wide in some places, up to fifteen feet in others. It starts at the edge of the crater and runs downhill about a thousand feet. Then the two sides come together, and it ends.

We call it The Crease because that's what my mother called it the first time she ever saw it, and the name stuck.

I kept going downhill till I came to a sunny, open meadow. I'd been there many times before. It was flat and full of tall grass, and it was surrounded by pines and aspens. Pheasants seemed to like it.

I did what my father always tells me to do: Try to think like a pheasant.

If I were a pheasant, I would like this meadow because it has lots of seeds and insects and berries, and sometimes lizards. Pheasants like lizards, if they're not too big. But if I were a pheasant, I wouldn't land in this meadow if I smelled anything dangerous. Like me.

A light breeze was blowing toward the small grove of aspens at the other end of the field. That would be my place. With the wind blowing toward me, no bird landing in the field would smell me. To make sure I left no scent in the field, I walked around the edge.

Not only does a pheasant not want to smell a human, he doesn't want to see one. So, I went to my favorite spot, behind a big rock near the edge of the grove. I notched a good arrow on my bowstring and crouched behind the rock. I stayed still, trying to become a part of it.

I didn't see any birds, or hear any, and as I waited I found myself thinking about Deputy Summerfield. Adam Summerfield. In a way, we were very much alike, because we were both young. I thought of us as girl and boy, even though he was older than I was and should probably be called a man.

I wondered what it was like to be a man like Adam. To be taller, have a different-shaped body, look at the world from a different point of view. Or was his view all that different? When Adam looked at me, for example, did he see just another person, but one who happened to be female? Or did he feel a pleasant little quiver inside, the way I did when I looked at him?

Someday I would want to be married, like my mother and father. I knew I wanted to have a family, but who would I marry? I'd met three young men in Badwater, but Adam Summerfield was the only one I'd want to even talk to again. But marry him? How could someone marry the first young man she'd ever met?

A bird called, a coarse sound. A magpie was flying off into the branches of a pine on the far side of the field. High above, a hawk circled. But after fifteen or twenty minutes he flew off to the south. I heard blue jays, but I couldn't see them.

I wished I'd met a girl in Badwater. Someone who saw boys all the time, knew all about them, and could tell me things. I wasn't sure what I wanted to know exactly. I just wanted to talk about them.

The sun was not yet overhead when a cock pheasant flew back and forth high over the field, as though he were looking it over. My heart beat a little faster.

The cock flew away. A breeze ruffled the field. The magpie called. My heart slowed to its normal beat.

I began to feel hungry. Just as I started wondering if I should get some deer jerky out of my pack, I heard a great whirring of wings. The cock pheasant was back, followed by three hens. I got excited, but I didn't move. The birds circled the field and landed.

I inched my bow to the top of the rock.

The grass was too deep for me to see the pheasants, but I could see the grass moving. The birds made low gabbling noises.

I listened carefully. It seemed like the cock pheasant was probably on the left side of the group, with the hens following him.

I stood up very slowly and aimed my arrow at the left side of the moving grass. I hoped the breeze would push the grass aside so I could see part of the bird.

I stood there a long time, my arrow at full draw.

A gust blew a break in the grass.

I caught a glimpse of the cock and let the arrow go.

Three birds whirred into the air. All hens.

There was no movement in the grass, except the wind.

I had my first bird.

I got a new arrow ready and ducked back down. I waited, listening to the aspens blow, go silent, blow some more.

It took a while before the three hens came over the field again. Two soared to the pines at the other end, then back to where the cock pheasant lay. They settled to the ground. The third hen flew off out of sight.

I rose again, slowly. I pulled my arrow to full draw and waited.

The magpie gave a raucous cry. It must have spooked the

hens, because they shot straight up. I released my arrow and one hen dropped. The other headed toward the pines, then came back and hovered above the spot where the other two birds lay.

I let a third arrow go.

The hovering hen shot up. My arrow whistled into the aspens as the hen flew directly over my head and disappeared.

I didn't believe either of the hens would return, so I decided to collect the other birds and try another place.

I picked up my gear and went to pick up the cock pheasant.

With no barbs, the arrow came out easily. The bird's breast and tail feathers were beautiful. I put him in the game bag.

The hen was beautiful in her own way. Not colorful, but not ordinary, either. I pulled out the arrow and put her in the bag.

I wondered what the other two hens would do. Would they find another cock pheasant? I hoped so.

I wiped the blood off my arrows with a handful of grass and set off toward the pines to find the arrow that had missed its target. I found it easily, its point dug into the shallow earth.

As I pulled it out, my eye caught something else. Something unfamiliar. Something shocking.

A leather glove!

A chill ran through my body. I had never, ever seen anything on the volcano that didn't belong to me, Father, or Lorraine.

Never.

This glove did not belong to any of us. It was a man's glove, too big for women. I shivered. Was someone in the forest with me? That seemed impossible. Yet here was proof that a stranger had been on the volcano.

Was he still here? I tried to think what to do.

Then I remembered my father's advice. Be invisible. Be careful. Keep your eyes and ears open. Hunt as though you're being hunted.

I crouched behind a rock outcrop near the edge of the pines and searched the meadow for movement. I had never looked at anything as hard as I was looking now.

Nothing.

I turned and looked over the top of the outcrop, scanning the field, searching the aspens beyond.

One of the hen pheasants flew back over the field and landed. I didn't move.

I knew I should tell my father as soon as possible. He would know what to do.

I thought about the sheriff's two drifters. Murderers, he had said. Had they somehow drifted up our volcano?

I took a long look into the aspen grove again. Still no movement. I put the glove in my pack and headed home.

What did this glove mean? Had someone besides me discovered this was a good field for hunting? But where would he come from? Badwater was much too far away to come for a bird hunt.

Was he hunting something else?

NINE

Father was coming up from the barn area, carrying a load of wood for the fire.

"How was the hunting?" he asked.

"Two birds," I said. "I quit because I found something you should see."

We walked into the big room. He set the wood down by the fireplace. "What is it?" he said.

I opened my pack and handed him the glove.

He examined it carefully. He looked at the front, then the back. He held it up against his own hand to gauge the size of the hand that had worn it.

He looked inside the glove. He smelled it. He smelled the outside, one finger at a time.

"Where'd you find it?" he asked.

"You know the meadow—below The Crease and a little

north. With the pines and the aspens? I was looking for an arrow when I found it."

Father felt the texture of the glove, its thickness. "Store-bought, obviously," he said. "Man's."

I nodded.

He looked at the glove thoughtfully. "Not good," he said.

I didn't say anything.

"In sixteen years," he said, "ever since your mother and I found this spot, I've never seen a trace of anyone on the volcano."

"Except Lorraine," I said.

"Except Lorraine." Then he said, "And Old Dan, a long time ago."

Lorraine came in and Father showed her the glove. "Katie-Bird found it."

Lorraine looked it over as carefully as my father had. She didn't say anything and handed it back.

"Someone from town might have tracked us, I suppose," Father said.

"Possible," Lorraine said.

"Nobody's ever come here before," I said. "So why now?"

I hoped I didn't know the answer.

Lorraine looked thoughtful. "I can think of a pretty good reason."

Father didn't say anything.

"Who else has been going to Badwater off and on for fifteen years, and every now and then exchanging gold coins for currency?"

"I know that's not a good thing to do," Father said, "but how else can I get paper money so we can buy what we need?"

"Not many people have gold these days, Jack," Lorraine said. "Bank people probably talk like everyone else."

"It's funny," my father said. "I was talking to Barton, the man who does the money-changing, nice fellow, he's been doing it at least ten years. Anyhow, he said he had another customer, someone who lives near Tenspike. That's where I've been saying I come from all these years. So he asked this fellow if he knew me. The fellow said no. Said he'd lived in the Tenspike area thirteen years, knew everyone around, but he'd never heard of me."

"What'd you tell him, Jack?" Lorraine asked.

"I said I lived pretty far west," Father said. "I asked him the fellow's name. He said Hungerford. I said I'd heard the name, but never met him. Of course, I've never heard the name Hungerford in my life."

Nobody said anything.

"I doubt Barton believed me," he said.

He put his elbows on his knees and rubbed his eyes. "I'm never really sure I haven't been tracked. As Katie knows, I keep a sharp eye, but how can you know for sure?"

We were all silent for a long time.

"I knew we couldn't stay hidden forever," Father said. "I just hoped it wouldn't come this soon."

He turned to me. "It's very important you found this. It serves as a warning for all of us."

"How far away did you find it?" Lorraine asked.

"North of The Crease," I explained. "You know, that field with the pheasants."

"Finding the glove doesn't mean the owner knows we're here, Jack," Lorraine said.

"It's not like finding it on our front step," he said, "but it's still a jolt." He laid the glove on the side of the fireplace.

"Well," he said, "we may not like finding a glove on our private volcano, but Katie found one anyway. So what do we do now that's different?"

"Be more careful than ever," Lorraine said. "Do more of that scanning in every direction when we go out hunting, I suppose."

"If we only had some way to signal one another when we go out," my father said. "Then if one of us ran into trouble, we could let the other two know. Then we could at least try to do something about it."

"Sometimes we get so spread out, Jack—like Katie hunting today—the only sound that would carry that far would be a gunshot," Lorraine said.

"We only have one gun," I said. "We'd need two more."

My father walked over to the fireplace and started building a fire.

"Maybe we could keep the new gun hidden in the cabin in a place we all know," he said, "and if any of us saw a person, or anything worrisome or suspicious, he or she would hightail it back to the cabin and fire the gun. That would be the signal to get back to the cabin fast—and very carefully."

"Wouldn't the shot tell the intruder where the cabin is?" I asked.

"If he's close enough that one of us has seen him, he'll find us anyway," my father said. "We leave tracks—impossible not to—and they all lead right to our door."

"It would at least let him know we're armed and dangerous," Lorraine said. "That might not do any harm."

Father took a deep breath, exhaled.

"Let's all sleep on it," he said. "Now, how about those birds?"

"I'll go fix them," I said.

"I shot a bird yesterday," Father said. "A dove. It's already cleaned. You can add it to the pot."

I took my game bag down the slope to our bird-cleaning spot. The cock pheasant was just as beautiful as before, but somehow it didn't mean as much.

I kept thinking: What would I do if I saw this person on the volcano? The very thought of it shook me up. It was a man, we knew that. But what kind of man? Was he just out hunting? Was he one of the outlaws the sheriff warned us about? Who was he, and what did he want, coming all the way up our volcano?

TEN

As summer wore on, I thought less and less about the glove. I still felt an occasional tremor when I remembered the sheriff's drifters, but the beauty of the summer, the wildflowers, the brilliant green of the trees seemed to push it all to the back of my mind.

We had decided to use the gun as a signal, and the loaded revolver was hidden under a small wooden box on a table near the front door. Firing it once meant come as fast as you can. Twice meant come fast but be extra careful, someone is near the cabin.

I spent a lot of time working on a new lemonwood bow and fletching a whole set of new arrows. My father advised me on both these projects, but he never touched them. He wanted me to do everything myself.

I had just finished the last of a dozen arrows when Father

walked up. He picked up one of the new arrows and sighted along it, inspecting the feathers.

"Very nice," he said.

"Thanks."

"Arrows this nice ought to be out looking for birds," he said. "Want to see what we can find?"

"Sure," I said. I loved hunting with him.

"Want to come, Lorraine?" my father called.

"You two go," she answered. "I've got some mending."

It was a beautiful day. Sunny but cool. We started north, toward The Crease, as we had done many times before. We angled downhill on our special path, then turned north again where The Crease ended.

We came to the meadow where I'd been hunting the day I found the glove. We crossed it and went through a thick stand of aspens to a second meadow with trees on three sides. The uphill side had a wall of rock.

"No point in two mighty hunters in the same field," Father said. "You stay here, I'll go to a place I like farther down."

"Okay," I said. "I'll be on the other side, downwind."

"See you in an hour or so," he said. "Less if I get lucky."

He walked off, and I began looking for a spot from which to shoot.

I have a favorite hunting rock in this meadow, too. Since the wind was right, I went straight to it. It's about four feet high, wide, with a top smooth enough to lean on comfortably and still keep a watch for birds.

I took my position, put an arrow on my bowstring, and kept perfectly still.

A breeze ruffled the grass. A blue jay squawked. I couldn't see him, but it didn't matter. I wasn't hunting blue jays.

A small covey of quail landed at the other end of the field. Too far for a shot. Besides, if I got one quail, the rest would scatter, and one quail doesn't make much of a meal.

I waited, watching, listening, but nothing came. It felt as though a long time had passed, but it always feels that way when you're waiting.

Then there was a cry, almost like a human cry.

A wild turkey!

A big turkey would feed us handsomely for two or three days!

I switched to a heavier arrow. If I got a shot, I didn't want the turkey running away wounded.

He cried again. Not a pretty sound. Half screech, half squawk. I couldn't tell if he was coming toward me or going away.

All was quiet. Had he noticed me?

Then I saw him. He walked majestically across the other end of the field, where I'd seen the quail. He was coming toward me at an angle. He looked awkward, but I knew he could be speedy when he needed to, and he could fly. That was more than I could do.

He stopped, pecked the dirt, walked some more, pecked

some more. He looked around, went on walking. If he kept it up, I would soon have a shot.

After a few more stops to peck, he was within range. But I didn't want to shoot if he was going to come even closer. Each step toward me meant a better chance for my shot.

He stopped. Called again.

I stood up, pulled my bow to full stretch, let go.

The turkey screeched and leapt into the air. He came down in the tall grass. The grass jerked back and forth, stopped moving, and then moved again. I heard a final screech and the grass didn't move anymore.

I fitted another arrow to my bow and walked over. He was totally still. He was a big, handsome bird. I felt sad at having ended his life. I always feel that way when I shoot a living thing, a pheasant, a turkey, a deer. But then I think about my father and Lorraine and me. We have to eat every day of the year.

If it wasn't him, it would be some other beautiful thing.

So now we had dinner. There was no reason for either of us to hunt any longer, so I left the turkey where he was. We could pick it up on the way home.

I started downhill through the trees, thinking how happy my father would be with my turkey.

A rock gave way under my foot, and I plopped down awkwardly. I sat there for a minute, thinking: That's what happens when you try to hurry.

I got up, dusted the dirt off my pants, adjusted my pack, and started off.

Then came the shock.

A man.

Thirty feet away.

Looking at me.

How could I not have seen him!

I felt alarm and shame. I hadn't been hunting as though I was being hunted. I hadn't been scanning in all directions.

And there he was. Big, tall, heavy, wearing a brown leather jacket with lots of pockets, buckskin pants like mine, a leather hat that blended in with the trees.

He wore a leather belt filled with bullets, just like the sheriff's, and a gun in a holster.

We both stared. Neither of us spoke. After a moment he started to smile. It wasn't a nice smile.

I knew that look. It was Jess! Jess Starkey who'd beat me up in Badwater!

My heart pounded. I felt like throwing up.

"Well, well, well," he said. "It's my old friend the dummy."

If only my father were here! But he was still hunting. I had no way to signal.

"And you've got your little bow," Jess said. "And all your little arrows."

I was really scared. I tried to think. What would my father do in my place? He wouldn't run, that much was certain. Jess would shoot him.

What could I do?

Maybe he was just hunting, like I was. But his mocking tone implied it wasn't hunting he was up to. He was downhill,

I was uphill. That was to my advantage. But he was big and had a gun, and even with all Lorraine had taught me, I wasn't sure I could beat him again.

How could I protect myself? I had my bow, of course, strung and ready. No match for the gun.

Could I talk my way to safety? It was the only weapon I had.

"You're Jess," I said. "Right?"

"I knew right away you could talk, dummy," he said. He laughed his mocking laugh.

I didn't want to cross him. I tried to sound cheery. "Couldn't fool you!"

"I knew you were a girl, too, right from the start."

"You saw right through me," I said. "I'm a rotten actor."

He started walking up the hill toward me. "You made a lousy boy."

I didn't want him to come closer, but he kept coming.

"But you're not too bad as a girl," he said. He laughed his sick laugh again.

"What are you doing up here?" I asked. "Hunting? I got a good turkey a few minutes ago. A big one. Maybe you'd like to have it. Save you looking any further."

Jess stopped walking and cocked his head to one side. "Well, isn't that sweet," he said. "You're going to give me your turkey!"

"It's a big one. I can get another easy. You want it?"

He started toward me again. When he stopped, he was only a few feet away.

"Oh, I want something," he said. "Yes, I want something,

but it's not a turkey. No, sir, I didn't come all the way up here to get myself a turkey."

"What are you hunting, then?"

He ignored my question. "And I didn't come here that long, phony way you and your old man take. You think we're all a bunch of idiots, don't you?" He stuck his face up close.

I could feel his breath.

"I've known you and your old man lived somewhere up here for a long time," he said. "And your old man thinks he's so damn smart!"

His right hand hung loosely over his gun. "So where's your cabin, sweetheart?" he said. "I hear you keep lots of nice things there. Some of them pretty valuable, they tell me. You want to show me where it is?"

"Actually," I said, "I'm not going back to the cabin for a while, Jess. I'm having a day of hunting. Besides, if I give you my turkey—and I really do hope you'll take it—then I want to get another one for myself."

He wasn't even listening. "We got off on the wrong foot back in town, don't you think?" he said.

I didn't say anything.

"I think we ought to fix all that," he said. "Start over, get to know each other. You should take me to your cabin so we can get acquainted. Don't you think so?"

"I see you got your gun," I said. "I remember you talking about it with your friend. What kind did you get?"

"Aren't we talkative all of a sudden!" he said. "You don't give a damn what kind of gun I got."

I ransacked my brain. "Really, I am interested," I said. "I've never seen a gun up close." That was a lie, but lying seemed like a necessary tool that might save my life.

Jess pulled the gun out of its holster and held it up close to my face. "See it, baby doll?"

He put his thumb on the hammer and pulled it back. It was cocked now, ready to fire. I knew that much about guns now.

He waved it back and forth in front of me. He pretended to aim at something to his left. "Pow," he said.

He aimed at something to his right. "Pow."

He brought the gun back and pointed it at my head.

I was too scared to move.

He grinned hideously. "Pow."

Still grinning, he uncocked the hammer and put the gun back in his holster.

"Well, sweetheart," he said. "Since we're starting over fresh, when I ask for the bow this time, you give it to me, okay?"

I took a deep breath. "Okay."

"So give me the bow."

I took the bow off my shoulder and handed it to him.

With one end of the bow on the ground and the other in his hands, he stepped on the middle of the shaft. He pulled with his arms, pushed with his foot, trying to break it.

But it wouldn't break. If I hadn't been scared to death, I might have laughed. Jess didn't realize how tough cured lemonwood can be. It bends, all right, which is why it makes a good bow, but it takes a lot to break it.

This made him mad. He tossed the bow into the trees and held out his hand. "Give me the goddamn arrows."

I handed him the quiver. He took the arrows out and put them over his knee as though he was going to break them. Then he thought better of it and threw them after the bow.

He turned back and smiled his mocking smile. "Maybe before we go to your cabin, there's time for something else." He took a step closer. "You must be hot in that jacket, sweetheart. Here, I'll help you out."

He grabbed my leather jacket with both hands and tried to yank it open. One button popped off, two came undone. One button held. I tried to hold it closed, but he gave a furious jerk and the jacket came open.

Suddenly he charged me. He didn't butt with his head this time, he just threw his whole body at me. I slammed to the ground, and he fell on top of me.

The fall knocked the wind out of me. He was even heavier than I'd thought. He pinned my arms to the ground.

I struggled to get my breath. I tried to throw him off, but I couldn't. He wriggled his body upward until his head was right over mine. He put his mouth over mine and started kissing. It wasn't like a kiss, it was like an attack.

I tried to turn away, but he ground his face against mine and tried to force his tongue through my clenched teeth.

I finally shook my head free. "Get off!" I yelled.

He grabbed my head again with both hands and rubbed his mouth against mine.

For a moment my hands were free. I grabbed his wrists

and pulled. I twisted my body and tried to throw him off, but he was too heavy.

As I struggled, he fished a leather thong from his pocket. One end had a slipknot already tied in it.

I jerked my left hand away as he grabbed for it. I kept it away and punched the side of his head with my other fist.

I felt a hard slap on my face. "You little slut!"

He went after my left hand again and captured it. The knot slipped over it easily and he pulled it tight.

My other hand was still free. I tried to keep it as far away from him as I could, waving it around wildly. Jess put his left hand on my shoulder and methodically worked his grip down my arm until he reached my wrist. He wrapped the thong around it and bound my hands together with a quick knot.

I hit him on the top of his head with my tied hands.

He laughed.

Then he threaded a longer thong between the one holding my hands together, looped it around the base of a sapling, and made a knot.

My arms were stretched above my head, useless. I jerked as hard as I could, but nothing happened.

Lorraine's secret about kicking men had worked last time, but this time there was no chance. His body pressed me into the earth so hard I could barely move my legs.

I tried shaking from side to side. Nothing helped.

Jess grabbed my shirt with both hands and ripped it open. He was kneeling over me now.

"Well, lookee here!" he said. "This is more like it!"

He stopped talking and started breathing hard. His hands were shaking as he unbuckled his gun belt. He undid the buttons on his pants, began to rip at mine.

Suddenly his body straightened.

He looked surprised.

He gave a little cry.

As he started to crumple, I saw the arrow sticking out of his chest.

I gave a mighty twist to avoid his falling body and saw my father running toward me.

ELEVEN

Father jerked Jess off me, cut the thongs, closed my jacket, and took me in his arms.

"Katie, Katie, Katie," he said. "My God, what have I let happen?"

I cried as I had never cried before. I put my arms around my father and sobbed into his shoulder. I felt sick, shaken, dirty from contact with Jess's brutality. I wanted to go to sleep, sleep a long, long time, and wake up finding it was just another bad dream, like the dream of losing my father in the flood.

Why had this happened? What had I done to deserve it? Jess had bullied me down in Badwater, and I'd fought back. I could understand his anger at being humiliated by a girl, but was that enough reason to climb all the way up the volcano, and hunt me down, and mock me, and tie me up, and try to . . .

He'd said he'd heard something about valuable stuff in our cabin. Was that why he'd come? Did he just run into me by accident?

I knew what Jess had wanted to do to me. Lorraine had explained all that to me a couple of years ago. But Lorraine had described it as an act of love.

This was the farthest thing from love.

"Are you hurt, Katie?" Father asked.

I couldn't speak. I shook my head no.

"You sure?"

I sobbed, swallowed, somehow managed to say, "I'm okay." I pressed my face into his coat again.

One thong still dangled from my wrist. Father cut it with his knife.

We sat there a long time, my father comforting me. Finally, I took a deep breath and looked up at him. "Thank you for saving me."

He held me to him very hard. "Katie, Katie, Katie."

For a while he said nothing. Then he relaxed his grip. "I knew something was wrong," he said. "I had a very bad feeling. It just hit me all of a sudden, and I knew I had to get back as fast as I could."

He shook his head, as though to clear it. "The closer I got, the more I knew you were in trouble. Then I saw this beast kneeling over you. I shot without even thinking."

"Thank you, Father," I said.

He got up and went over to Jess's body.

I stood up and began buttoning my shirt. Suddenly I felt

panicky. I thought I was going to cry again. I took deep breaths until the panic went away.

I started to button my coat. Two buttons were missing. I looked around and found them on the ground. I put them in my pocket.

I couldn't stop thinking about Jess. If he hated me, why didn't he just kill me? He had a gun. There's no way I could have got away. All he had to do was pull the trigger.

Father was looking down at Jess, lying on his back, his eyes wide open.

"Why, this is the same no-good we saw down in Badwater!" he said.

I nodded.

Father was still glaring down at Jess. For a moment I thought he was going to kick him.

"Son of a bitch!" he said.

I had seen my father angry only once before, after the fight down in Badwater. He was annoyed, maybe, when a piece of harness broke or something like that, but not like this. I had never heard him swear.

He took a deep breath, and let it out.

"He wanted to find our cabin," I said. "He said he'd heard we keep valuable things there."

My father snorted. "He did, did he?"

"I think he heard about our gold."

Father knelt beside Jess and rolled him onto his side. The feathered shaft of the arrow stood straight out from his back. He pushed it forward and back, but it wouldn't loosen.

He took out his hunting knife and cut the shaft off. Then he reached around Jess's body and cut off the pointed part sticking out of his chest.

"Never leave stuff lying around," Father said as he put both parts of the arrow into his quiver.

"Do you suppose that other lowlife was with him? This one doesn't strike me as brave enough to come up here alone." He stood still a moment, thinking. "We'd better check."

Father lifted Jess's left boot and began to study the sole.

"What are you doing?" I asked.

"We have to track him downhill a ways," he said, "and I want to see if his soles or heels have any cuts or scars. Makes it easier to track him if they do."

He studied the right boot. "A nicked sole is like a signature," he said. "You sign your name every step you take."

"So do his boots have any cuts?" I said.

"They're too new," he said. "We just have to hope that if he came with his friend, his friend's boots have a different sole. Or they're old and have had a hard life. Or he wore moccasins. So we can tell them apart."

Father saw my bow and arrows lying in the brush and brought them to me. He put his arm around my shoulders and gave me a squeeze.

"You up for this, Katie-Bird?" he asked.

I nodded. I needed something to think about other than what had just happened. I was truly shaken. If I concentrated on tracking, I wouldn't have to think about anything else.

My father pointed at Jess's tracks. "Let's go."

The ground was dry, so the tracks were faint. To me, they were hard to follow. To my father, they were a hand-drawn map.

We followed them downhill for nearly an hour, until they led into a grassy clearing with the remains of a campfire. Farther out in the field was an old gelding, saddled, hobbled, trailing his reins as he grazed the short grass. He looked up at us briefly, then went back to grazing.

"Too lazy even to unsaddle his horse," Father said.

I looked back at the dead campfire and shuddered. In my mind I saw Jess, up the volcano behind us, lying on his back, eyes wide open, staring at the sky. I felt sick, angry, confused. I wanted it not to have happened.

"Careful," my father said as we approached the dead fire, "we don't want to mess up any tracks. These obviously belong to Jess." He pointed. "They're the same we've been following. And here's where he spread his bedroll."

Father moved to the other side of the fire. "Hey, take a look at this, Katie," he said. "What do you think?"

I moved to his side of the fire and examined the print. At first it looked like the prints we'd been following, but then I saw it.

"It's got a cut!" I said. "Sideways across the heel!"

He smiled at me. "You're going to be a good tracker."

I smiled a little.

"Well, now we've got two sets of tracks," he said, "but only one horse. How do you figure that?"

I suspected Father knew very well how to figure it but was testing me. "Maybe his friend went back to Badwater."

"Possible," he said.

"We should check the horse tracks," I said. "There must be two sets coming up. Let's see if any are going down."

Father looked pleased.

It was easy finding two sets of horses' tracks coming up the volcano. And sure enough, we found one set of tracks going back downhill. My father thought they looked about a day old.

We followed them far enough to satisfy ourselves the rider wasn't just shifting campsites. Then we went back to the clearing and the grazing horse.

The horse looked up as we approached. My father spoke softly to him, stroked his neck, rubbed his nose.

"We'll send him home." He picked up the trailing reins and tied them loosely over the horse's neck.

Father led the horse to where they'd come up. He pointed him downhill and gave him a friendly pat on the rump. "Go home, boy," he said. "They've got some good food for you there."

The horse looked back over his shoulder, doubtful.

"Go on, boy," he said.

The horse turned and began picking his way downhill. We started climbing back to where we'd left Jess.

When we got there, nothing had changed. Jess lay on his back, staring at the sky.

Father bent over and closed Jess's eyes. "Well," he said, "we've got some work to do."

I looked at the body. Motionless. Heavy.

"What are we going to do with him?" I asked.

"We'll get Billy."

He knelt beside Jess and took the gun from the holster. He opened it, checked the bullets, and closed it. He put it in the side pocket of his own jacket. The bullets from Jess's belt went there, too.

Then he emptied Jess's trouser pockets and laid the contents on the ground. A pocketknife. A large, ragged piece of cloth. A box of bullets.

He put the bullets into his pocket with the gun. A comb. Two keys, tied together with a string. A short, sturdy bolt with the nut screwed on.

One of Jess's pockets held a small, flat can.

"What's that?" I asked.

"Snuff," my father said.

His jacket pocket held a leather envelope containing Territorial paper money and a metal whistle.

From the inside pocket of the jacket he took out a thick, silvery disk. He whistled and held it out toward me.

My magnifying glass!

It was mine, all right. I saw my mother's initials on the side, S.T.

A shudder ran through my body. It was my glass, but I didn't want to handle it. Jess had carried it, used it. Contaminated it.

"I'll look after it," my father said. He put it in his pocket.

He put everything else back into Jess's pockets. "He must have a pack somewhere."

We found it in about ten minutes.

It held food, a sweater, a blanket rolled very tight, odds and ends. My father put everything back and tossed the pack alongside Jess's body.

For a long time he just stood there, staring down at the body. Finally, he said, "Well, let's get going."

As we crossed the meadow where I'd been hunting, I picked up my turkey. I'd been so pleased when I'd shot it. Now it didn't seem to matter.

Still, it was dinner. No matter what happened this day or any other day, we still had to eat.

I held it up.

My father's grim face softened a little. "Good job," he said.

Back at the cabin, Father told Lorraine what had happened.

Lorraine put her arms around me and didn't say anything. She just held me there, tightly, the way my father had. I felt the tears come again.

After a while I said, "I'm okay, Lorraine," and she relaxed her grip.

"You're a strong woman, Katie," she said.

"There were two of them," my father said. "One apparently went back yesterday. The one who's dead was apparently looking for our gold."

Lorraine came with us when we went back to the body.

My father led Billy, and Lorraine carried a big coil of rope. I just carried my bow, slung over my shoulder, and my quiver.

As we walked, we heard the volcano talking to itself. Quiet at first, then a faint, deep grumbling noise that seemed to come from the middle of the earth. Louder, louder, a muffled boom, then silence.

When we reached Jess, my father tied one end of the rope just under his armpits. He sat the body up, and he and Lorraine tied the arms against the body and tied the legs together. Then they each lifted one side and laid Jess's body across Billy's back, facedown. I passed the rope under Billy's stomach and Father tied it to Jess's feet and snugged it up. He tied Jess's pack behind the body.

"Where are we taking him?" I asked.

My father finished his final knot. "The Crease."

I led Billy. My father and Lorraine walked alongside, making sure Jess didn't slip.

We passed the bottom of The Crease and turned straight uphill.

Halfway to the crater we stopped. Billy waited as the three of us looked down into The Crease.

It was about eight feet wide at that point. There was no way you could see the bottom. My father picked up a rock, held it out over the edge, and let it go. It banged against the sides, then went out of sight. We never heard it hit bottom.

"What do you think?" he asked.

He was looking at Lorraine, but then he looked at me, as though he wanted my opinion, too.

"Good," Lorraine said.

"We don't want him getting hung up on the sides," he said.

"Looks smooth as far as I can see," she answered.

My father turned to me. "Katie?"

I took another look down the deep, narrow slot. "Looks smooth," I agreed.

"Okay, let's do it," Father said.

All the things we'd done when we loaded Jess, we now did in reverse. My father laid Jess's pack on the ground, and he and Lorraine eased Jess off Billy's back. They set the body parallel to the edge of The Crease.

"Okay," Father said to Lorraine, "you take the feet. I'll take under the arms."

They picked the body up.

"On the count of three," my father said.

They looked at each other and began to swing the body from side to side.

"One . . . two . . ."

They gave a mighty swing.

"Three!"

Jess flew out to the center of The Crease and dropped noiselessly out of sight.

It felt very strange. One minute there'd been a body there—a young man named Jess. Now there wasn't.

My father tossed Jess's bag into The Crease. He took the

severed arrow ends out of his quiver and tossed them in after the bag.

He looked at the rope. One end was bloody, so he cut that off and tossed it in, too.

All three of us examined the ground carefully. We wanted to make sure we hadn't left anything.

"Okay," my father said, "let's go home."

TWELVE

When we were back inside the cabin, nobody wanted
to talk.

Father broke the silence. "I have your magnifying glass,
Katie. I'm going to give it a thorough cleaning and polish it.
Then I'll give it to you. I know you don't want it now."

Jess had handled it. Jess had carried it. Jess had attacked me.

It had belonged to my mother, not to Jess, but I didn't even
want to touch it.

I had to think about it.

"Thanks, Father," I said. "I don't think I'll start carrying it
right away. Maybe if you'd just put it in the bowl. I know I'll
go back to using it, but not just now."

I was talking about the wooden bowl we keep in the center
of the big table. It holds little things we don't want to lose.
Sometimes it's a screw to be put back in a piece of furniture,

or a harness buckle, or sometimes it's just a pretty rock one of us found.

"I understand," my father said.

"I'll go fix the bird," I said.

I took the turkey down to the plucking bench and sat down. I didn't know what to think. My mind was reeling. The day had started out so ordinary. Fletching arrows. Hunting with my father. And then the horrible, horrible episode with Jess. Then using Billy to take Jess up to The Crease. And dropping him in. Getting rid of him. And then back to ordinary. Plucking a turkey.

It was too much for one day, too much to think about. But I knew I would probably think about it the rest of my life. How could I forget it?

As wild turkeys go, this was a fat one. He took a long time to pluck, and when I finished, I gutted him and took him up to the big room to roast.

Lorraine had stirred up the fire. She helped me rub the turkey with fat and put it on the spit. Together we put the spit over the coals.

My father had made a device so we could turn the spit sitting down. He rigged it up, and I sat down and began to turn the spit slowly.

None of us had much to say. We just sat there, listening to the creak of the spit.

After a while Lorraine took over on the spit. I went down to the barn and brushed Billy and cried.

My feelings were all mixed up. I didn't know why I was

crying. I was safe. I wasn't hurt. My father had saved me. My father loved me, Lorraine loved me. I lived in a nice cabin, I had food to eat, a good place to sleep, books I liked to read.

None of that had changed, yet I couldn't stop crying. My life was somehow different now. Jess had made it different.

I finished brushing Billy and started on Valerie. I'd stopped crying, but all I could think of was Jess. Tying me up. Leering over me.

And now he was dead.

Jess was dead because of me.

This morning there had been a man living on this earth named Jess Starkey. Now there wasn't. My father had killed him. Killed him because Jess Starkey was trying to harm his daughter. Jess Starkey would never shoot his new gun again, never walk the boardwalks of Badwater again, never see his friend again.

All because of me.

What had I done wrong?

Maybe I should never have gone to Badwater.

I felt sorry for Jess. I wished it had never happened. I wished he had never come up the volcano. I wished, I wished, I wished. But what good were wishes? Jess Starkey was dead. He was out of wishes.

Valerie liked being brushed just as much as Billy. I kept brushing, brushing, brushing, and she made snorting noises that meant she was happy.

Should I feel guilty because Jess was dead? No. I didn't do anything to him.

So, why did I feel so bad?

When I finished with Valerie, I rubbed my eyes on my sleeve and took a cloth out of my pocket and blew my nose. Then I went back up to the cabin.

My father was turning the spit with one hand when I came into the big room. Lorraine was sitting beside him, holding his other hand.

"I brushed the horses," I told them.

"Good," my father said.

"Thanks, Katie," Lorraine said.

Usually it was easy to talk during dinner, but this night was different. The turkey was delicious, but no one seemed to have much to say.

After we'd cleared the dinner things, we went out onto the porch and watched the shadow spread over the crater.

As it got darker, Lorraine said good night and went indoors.

A few minutes later my father stood up, and so did I. He put his arms around me and pressed my head against his chest. For a long time he just held me.

Neither of us said a word.

The next morning at breakfast my father said, "We have to talk about this thing."

We all knew what the thing was.

"I'll start," he said. "I'm sorry that young man is dead." He paused and looked at me, then Lorraine. "I know we're all sorry. But he was about to hurt you, Katie. Maybe kill you. I was forty, fifty yards away, I guess. I didn't think I could get there in time. So, I shot him. I'd do the same thing today. But I'm still sorry he's dead."

"You couldn't have done anything else, Jack," Lorraine assured him.

"These things have many sides," my father said. "He probably has a father and a mother down in Badwater who don't even know he's dead yet. They think he's out hunting."

Nobody said anything.

"Once upon a time he was an innocent little baby in a crib," Father said. "So what happened?"

"I don't know, Jack," Lorraine said.

I turned and looked at the sunlight pouring in the door.

"Well, that's all I wanted to say," my father said.

We were all quiet for a few moments.

"I'm sorry he's dead, too," I said. "But I'm glad you saved me, Father."

Inside my head I heard Jess talking. *Where's your cabin, sweetheart?*

"I was tied up," I continued, "and there wasn't anything I could do."

I heard Jess again. I was trying to fight him off. *This is more like it.*

I caught my breath.

"It's lucky you're a good shot, Jack," Lorraine said.

My father patted her arm.

"No." Lorraine shook her head. "It wasn't luck at all. You had to make the shot. So you made it."

Father walked to the door and looked out. It was hot in that wonderful late-summer way. He came back and stood by the table.

"Before long, someone's going to miss him down in Badwater," he said. "Some family member, some friend. And then what? Will they come looking for him?"

"They'll never find him," Lorraine answered. "We may never even hear about him again."

"Don't I wish!" Father exclaimed. "But somebody will come, Lorraine. There's no way we can stop them."

"It's a long trip from Badwater," Lorraine said. "And it's not exactly as though there's a trail leading here."

"If Jess Starkey can find his way, someone else can," he said.

We all thought about that a few moments.

"I've got his gun and his ammunition," my father said. "So now we have two guns. Let's think about how to work a second gun into our signaling system and how else we can use it to make ourselves safer. If Jess Starkey came up here to sniff out our gold, you can bet your boots some other sniffers will come before long."

Lorraine and I nodded. We both knew it was true.

Father took a tiny deerskin bag from his pocket and poured out three golden coins onto the table. "I was going to change these for paper money when you and I were down there, Katie. Things kind of got out of hand, so I didn't get around to it. It doesn't matter, because I've got enough paper money to last awhile. I don't think we should keep any gold in the cabin anymore, though, so I'm going to put these coins back with the rest. Why don't we all go, just to refresh everyone's memory about where we keep them. Katie, you bring a trowel and a bucket."

Lorraine and I followed Father down past the barn and the cool house, into a clearing surrounded by a thick grove of aspens.

"All right, Katie, where do they go?" my father asked.

I started counting aspen trees to the left from where we had entered the grove.

When I got to the seventh tree, I walked to the third aspen directly behind it.

"Here," I said. "Seven and three."

"Good work," my father said. "You might as well dig it up."

And so I did. I dug down about six inches, carefully saving the dirt in the bucket, until I hit metal. Under this flat piece of metal was a hole lined with wood to keep dirt from falling in, and inside the hole was a cylindrical metal container. I lifted it out—it was heavy—and handed it to my father. He unscrewed the top and dropped the little buckskin bag inside. He screwed the top back on, and I lowered the cylinder back into the hole.

I replaced the top, filled the hole with dirt from the bucket, and packed it down. Then I got a couple of handfuls of dried dirt from a few trees away and spread it around. I sprinkled some leaves over it and stepped back.

"Perfect, Katie-Bird," Father said, and we all trooped back up to the cabin.

We all felt better after we'd had our talk and buried the coins. We didn't feel right yet, just better.

As time went on, it got easy to talk again. We didn't forget about what happened, we couldn't. But we went about our chores with lighter hearts.

THIRTEEN

The next day, all three of us went down to the barn to fix the hinges on one of the doors. It was one of those jobs where one person lifts, one pushes, and one screws a nut on a bolt.

When we came back up to the cabin, we found a great surprise. Sitting on our front porch, his pack by his side, was an old man in white buckskins.

"Dan!" my father called. He hurried toward the porch.

The old man got up from the bench slowly.

"Daniel Mills! It's wonderful to see you!"

Dan smiled and held out his hand. "Hello, Jack."

They took their time shaking hands, as though neither believed it could be happening.

"Hello, Dan," Lorraine said.

"Lorraine," Dan said. "Pretty as ever. I hoped I'd find you here."

Lorraine gave the old man a kiss on the cheek.

"How long has it been?" my father asked. "Ten years? No, more than that."

"Fourteen," Dan replied. "It was when they was still shooting each other up down in the flat."

"Dan," Father said, "you remember that little girl who was running around when you were here last? Well, this is Katie. All grown up now. Katie, you probably don't remember when Dan Mills came, do you?"

"I remember your buckskins," I said.

He walked over and shook my hand. Up and down, up and down. "So you remember me from all those years ago." He shook his head. "Well, what do you know."

Lorraine roasted some venison for dinner. I got the chair out of my room for Dan to sit on. Afterward, we sat around the table a long time, talking.

"Look at that," Dan said. He reached into the bowl and lifted out my magnifying glass. It was all clean and shiny.

"I remember this," he said. He turned to my father. "Belonged to Sarah, didn't it?"

"Belongs to Katie now," my father said.

Dan opened it, closed it gently, put it back in the bowl, and smiled at me.

I liked how Dan handled it. Maybe I would start carrying it again one of these days.

Mostly, I just listened that night. I learned things I'd never known before. I learned that Dan had known my father ever since he was born. He'd been a friend not only to my father, but my grandfather as well.

I listened carefully while Dan told stories about surviving on the land. All by himself. Once, he said, he'd had a wife named Isabella and two sons. They'd lived just outside a town in New Pacifica. When the fighting came, it quickly swept through their town and everything near it. Dan had been away trapping muskrat. He came back to find his family dead.

"That was a terrible crime," my father said. "It was the kind of immoral, outrageous act that drove me and Sarah out of Little Fish. And even though things have calmed down quite a bit, it's not completely over. That's why we still try to stay hidden up here on our volcano."

Since losing his family, Dan had traveled alone. He stayed away from towns. When he needed someone or something really badly, then he had to go into a town and meet up with people again. But he didn't like it.

Mostly, he'd lived in forests like ours, or in deserts, or beside the ocean. He liked the ocean because it was so clean. He liked the smell. He said he took baths in it, but you couldn't drink it, it was too salty. I tried to picture an ocean. All that water, as far as you could see. I couldn't imagine what it would be like.

When it got late, my father said, "Dan, I want you to do me a favor and sleep in our bed. I doubt you've seen too many beds lately, and it would make us feel good to know we could make you comfortable."

"I wouldn't know what to do in a bed anymore," Dan said. "Thanks, Jack, but I'd probably fall out and scare the horses."

"It's a big, comfortable bed, Dan," Father said. "You won't fall out."

"No," Dan replied. "If it's not raining or snowing, I prefer sleeping out. I like it. So, if you don't mind, I'll just put my bedroll on your porch. I'll be asleep before you know it."

The next day we all took it easy. We sat on the porch and soaked up the sun. There wasn't a cloud in the sky, and for once there wasn't a trace of smoke from the volcano.

We talked, we dozed, we looked out across the crater. At one point my father went down to the barn, and Lorraine went into the cabin, and it was just Dan and me sitting there.

"Dan, did you know my mother?" I asked.

Dan turned away from the crater and looked directly at me. "Yes, I knew your mother. Sarah. I knew her from a little girl."

I felt a pulse of excitement when Dan said my mother's name. "What was she like?"

He considered a moment. "She was a fine woman," he said. "Very smart. Fair-minded. Generous. She'd help anyone who needed it."

I didn't say anything. I hoped he'd go on.

"She had a nice sense of what was funny. I always liked that about her."

My father had said the same thing. I loved hearing that.

"She was brave, too." Dan nodded. "She had to be brave to leave what they called civilization in those days and come out to these parts with your dad. I had a lot of respect for your mother."

Brave. I liked that.

"She was real pretty, too. When I look at you, I see a lot of her. Same eyes. Same smile. Same color hair. You could be her twin."

I leaned back and looked out over the crater. I looked like my mother.

That night, after we'd cleared dinner, Dan said, "Katie, you want to see my collection?"

"Sure," I answered. "Your collection of what?"

"Oh, just stuff," he said. "Things I've picked up here and there that I happen to like. I've had some of it fifty years."

Dan went to his pack and got out a big leather pouch. We all four sat down at the big table as he undid the braided leather cord that held it closed.

I thought he'd just turn the pouch upside down and let his things tumble out. Instead, he peered in, stuck his hand in, felt around, and finally brought something out.

He buffed it up and down on the front of his shirt and then laid it carefully in the middle of the table.

It was a polished stone, round as a ball, just big enough to hold in your hand with your fingers mostly closed. It was black and had a lot of white lines going around it. Some of the lines were thick, some thin, some wavy. And the lines weren't just on the surface. You could see they went all the way through the stone. It was beautiful.

"That there's an agate," Dan said. "I've had that thing since I was a young man. I was up in the high mountains and I kicked this little block of stone. It was rough, but I could see it had a lot of beauty in it. So, I carried it with me a few years till I came to a town where there was a man who worked stones. I showed him my little block of agate and asked if he could carve something nice out of it. This is what he made."

Nobody touched it. We just looked.

"Go ahead, you can touch it," Dan said. "That's part of what's nice about it."

I picked it up. My father had taught me about the planets, how Saturn had rings, and now I felt as if I were holding a very small planet in my hand, only the rings went all the way through it.

Dan reached into his pouch again. This time he brought out a pocket watch with a chain.

"That looks like gold," my father said.

"You bet your boots, Jack," Dan said. "Gold watch, gold chain. I won't tell you how I come by it, except I didn't steal it. Here, Katie, have a look at this watch."

The watch was heavy, and the chain was heavy, too. I turned it over and thought I would see hands and numbers, but both sides were just smooth gold, with beautiful designs carved into them.

"Let me show you," Dan said. He reached over and touched the watch, and it opened up. The front was a little round door on a hinge. I wondered how anyone could make something so intricate and beautiful.

"Hand it around," Dan said, "and take a look at this."

This time he held another perfectly round thing. It was almost three times bigger than the agate, bone-colored, very smooth, and it looked very old. You could see a tiny line where it had been cut in half, straight through the middle. There was another line where one of the halves had been cut in half again.

"Open sesame," Dan said.

The two quarter pieces folded back on tiny gold hinges. The inside was carved out to make a scene of men fighting. There was a man on a rearing horse, and other men with swords and guns. "It's old, very old," Dan said. He laid it carefully on its back beside the agate and the watch. "It's some kind of battle. I don't know when it happened, and I don't know where. But I do know this ball is a piece of real ivory, and the man who spent his life carving its insides was a genius."

Before he was through, Dan showed us a gold ring with writing carved inside it and another gold thing he called a locket. It also opened up, and had a tiny picture of a woman inside.

"Isabella," my father said.

Dan nodded, just barely. He stared at the locket for a long moment, closed it, and laid it on the table.

He fished around in his bag again and pulled out a gold nugget. It was as big as the first joint of his thumb. He'd found it in a creek a long time ago.

"There it was, staring up at me in the middle of nowhere,

water rippling over it just as pretty as could be," he said. "Just waiting for me to pick it up."

The last thing he pulled from his pouch was a string of white stones. They were very smooth and beautiful.

"These here are pearls," he explained. "They come from out of the ocean. People dive down and bring up things called oysters, and they open 'em up and sometimes they find pearls in 'em."

He laid the pearls beside the locket. "Go ahead. Pick 'em up."

Lorraine reached for them. "Did you get these when you were living by the ocean?"

"Long before that," he said. "A fellow had 'em, and I had something the fellow wanted. Lucky for me he didn't know how bad I wanted the pearls. I wanted them for Isabella. So we haggled and finally struck a deal."

"I'll bet she loved them," Lorraine said.

"She never got to see 'em." Dan took the pearls back and held them in his hands. He looked at them silently.

"I'm sorry," Lorraine said.

"I know," Dan said. He laid the pearls on the table and very carefully began putting his things back in the pouch.

Finally, only the string of pearls lay on the table. Dan picked them up and held them by the ends. When he moved his hands together, the pearls hung in a loop.

Without taking his eyes from the pearls, he said, "Katie?"

"Yes," I answered.

"These are your pearls now," he said.

I sat perfectly still. I didn't know what to say.

"Take 'em," Dan said. "Jack, tell her it's okay."

My father looked at me. "It's okay, Katie."

I looked into Dan's eyes. They'd been blue once, I guessed. Now there was a lot of white mixed in with the blue.

"Thank you, Dan," I said. I took the pearls from his hands and held them. Lorraine reached over and took them. She stood behind me and held the pearls in front of my chest.

"Lift up your hair," she said.

I lifted my hair with both hands. Lorraine brought the ends of the strand together behind my neck and fastened the clasp.

"You can let it down now, Katie-Bird," she said.

I looked down at the pearls. I stood up and went over to the cracked mirror.

"Thank you," I said. I looked in the mirror again. "I can't believe it, Dan."

"Good," he said.

It's hard to explain how good Dan's pearls made me feel. Partly, it was because they were so beautiful. I'd read about ladies with pearls in one of my mother's books, but I'd never dreamed I'd ever see any, let alone have some of my very own. Wearing them made me feel older, more adult, more like a real woman.

There was something else about the pearls that made them especially endearing to me. Dan had bought them for Isabella, his wife. I felt there was a lot of love stored up in these pearls, love that now belonged to me.

I wore them to dinner every night as long as Dan was there.

Dan stayed with us for almost two weeks. Then after breakfast one morning he stood up and walked over to his pack.

"I'm leaving you good people today," he said. "You don't know what it means to see you all again. Seems we picked right up where we left off."

"Do you have to go, Dan?" Lorraine asked.

"Think I'd better," he answered. "It's good to see you, Katie, all grown up into a woman."

"Why go now?" my father asked. "Seems like you just got here."

"Well, thanks, Jack," Dan said. "I feel the same way. I know summer's still not quite over, but I've got a long ways to go to get to where I want to spend the winter. I used to like breaking trails through the snow, things like that, but now all I want is sunshine. If I get there early, so much the better. I'm through bedding down on frozen ground. I guess I've turned into a softy."

My father snorted. "Some softy."

FOURTEEN

With Dan gone, the cabin seemed kind of empty. All day I kept thinking about him and his stories. And that he had cared enough about the three of us to make the long journey to visit us.

Lorraine and I sat out on the porch after dinner that night, watching the light fade to nothing over the volcano.

After a while I broke the silence. "How do you know Dan, Lorraine?"

"I met him when I came out to the Territories with my husband," she said. "Dan was already here."

"Your husband!" I exclaimed. I sat up straight.

"I was married once," she said. "Ages ago."

"Where is he now?" I asked. "Your husband."

"He's dead," she said.

I was astonished. Lorraine had been married? She'd had a

husband, and now he was dead? Lorraine, who I knew so well? Maybe I didn't know her at all.

"Why didn't you ever tell me about this?" I asked.

"Well, some of it's not all that wonderful to tell. I thought it might be better to wait till you were older and might understand better."

"I'm sixteen now, Lorraine," I said. "Is that old enough?"

"Yes, it is, Katie-Bird, and I've been thinking about telling you," she said. "That's the truth. I guess I've been putting it off, because it's a little hard to get started."

"Let's start with his name. What was it?"

Lorraine paused a long time before answering. "Richard," she said. "Richard Carter. They called him Rick."

"What did he look like?"

"Oh, he was handsome," she said. "He was big, six feet tall, very strong, nice teeth, big smile."

"Was he nice?"

Again Lorraine took her time. "Not really."

"Oh," I said, surprised.

"Well, he was nice at first," she said. "Very nice. Too nice. And I was absolutely crazy about him. But later it turned out he had another side."

Lorraine stopped. She looked out over the crater. It was so dark I could hardly see her.

"You don't have to tell me, Lorraine. I shouldn't have asked."

"No," she said, "I want to tell you. I don't want any secrets from you, Katie. You mean too much to me."

I didn't say anything.

"He had a nasty side is what I mean," Lorraine said. "I never saw it before we were married. It came on him slowly at first, and just kept growing. It got worse when he drank."

"What kinds of things would he do?"

"Oh, he'd swear at me, threaten me, tell me how worthless I was." Lorraine paused. "Sometimes he'd hit me, beat me up."

"Oh, Lorraine." I couldn't imagine anyone hurting her. Dear, dear Lorraine, who was so loving, so generous, so helpful, whom I loved as a sister and sometimes as the mother I had never known. I felt very angry at Richard Carter, angry even though he was dead.

"That was when I started learning those things about defending myself that I've been teaching you." She paused for a moment.

"One night he got roaring drunk," she said quietly. "He came into our cabin swearing and kicking the chairs, and he knocked me down. Then he jumped on top of me, and I saw a hunting knife in his hand."

"A knife!"

"He slapped my face back and forth, and he cursed me, and then, laughing like a wild man, he cut my cheek, on purpose, all the way from my nose to my ear."

I gasped.

"You asked me once how I got that scar?" she said. "Well, that's how."

I couldn't believe it! "That's terrible, Lorraine, terrible!"

"He said that was just the beginning. He waved the knife

around and said he was going to carve me up like a Christmas turkey. He raised the knife high over me like he was going to plunge it into my throat."

She looked at her hands. It was very quiet.

I didn't want to ask, but I had to.

"What did you do?" I whispered.

Lorraine was silent so long I thought she wasn't going to answer. Then she spoke, very softly.

"I killed him."

I couldn't say a word.

"I managed to reach the sheath knife on my belt," she said, "and I drove it up into his belly, and held it there."

I got up and knelt in the darkness beside Lorraine. I put my arms around her and we were both silent for a long time.

"I didn't see what else I could do," she said, "if I wanted to live."

I stayed awake a long time that night, thinking about Lorraine. I thought about Richard Carter. How terrible Lorraine must have felt when she realized he was a dangerous beast. I felt sorry for all she had suffered, all the things I'd never known about.

I wondered if my father knew. Then I realized he must know. Lorraine would never keep secrets from him.

The next morning Lorraine and I walked down to the barn to see how Billy and Valerie were getting along.

"That wasn't a very nice story I told you last night,

Katie," she said. "I don't mind talking about it if you have questions."

"That couldn't have been easy for you to tell me, Lorraine," I said. "But I'm glad you did."

I did want to ask her one thing. "Did you get in any trouble?"

The horses nickered as we entered the barn.

"Nobody really missed Rick," Lorraine said. "We lived seven miles from our nearest neighbor. If anyone ever asked where he was, I said he'd gone back to New Pacifica. I buried him under a tree fifty yards from the house. Nice and shady. I guess I owed him that. But no marker."

I wondered what I would have done in Lorraine's place. Then I thought, in some ways this wasn't too different from what had happened with Jess Starkey. He was lying on top of me, pinning me down, he had a weapon, he was acting like a crazy man.

I'd had my hunting knife with me, but it was stowed in my pack. If I could have reached it, what would I have done? Would I have used it?

I thought about it a long time, and I still wasn't sure.

Later that morning, after my chores were done, I took the telescope out onto the porch. Summer had turned to autumn, and it was an exceptionally clear day, a good day to try to see the place where the volcano's smoke came out of the ground.

But I couldn't see it. It was hidden behind one of the many hills that rose from the underbrush and trees and streams of smooth black lava that made up the enormous crater floor. I looked at the far side of the volcano. Clear as the day was, I still couldn't make anything out.

I went indoors to make lunch and an idea came to me. A great idea. I could hardly wait to spring it on my father and Lorraine.

When the three of us were sitting down eating, I asked, "You know what I'd like us to do?"

"No," my father said, "but I have a feeling you're going to tell us."

"I'd like the three of us to hike all the way around the volcano," I said. "I figure it would take three days, maybe four. Five at the most."

Father smiled. He looked at Lorraine, then back at me. "Where on earth did that idea come from?"

"Well, you know how I've always wanted to see the other side?" I said. "You told me not to go alone. So, I figure if the three of us went together, it would be all right."

My father didn't say anything. Neither did Lorraine.

"Well, wouldn't it?" I asked.

Father laughed. "It sure would, but it's a long hike just to get back to where you came from."

"I want to see what's on the other side," I pleaded. "And maybe we could go down inside the crater. I'd like to get a look at where the smoke comes from."

"What do you think, Lorraine?" my father said.

Lorraine smiled at me. "I think Katie is young and full of energy."

"It's a good hike," Father said. "What is it, thirty-five, forty miles round trip?"

"That's not very far," I said.

"Don't forget the thrilling excursion into the crater," Lorraine said.

My father put on his thoughtful look. He turned to Lorraine, then back to me. "Well, why not? If you two want to go, I guess I can drag my carcass along."

"No, no, no, Jack." Lorraine shook her head. "Not me. You and the energetic Miss Katie-Bird go. I'll stay and look after the horses."

My father looked at me. "Well, Katie, how about a hike with your father?"

"You'll do it? Just the two of us?" I turned to Lorraine. "You should come, too. We'll have a wonderful time."

But Lorraine just sat there with her arms folded, smiling and shaking her head.

The next day we all did chores so Lorraine wouldn't have too much to do while we were away.

That night my father and I assembled our packs. Even though we were only planning to be gone five days at the most, we took a ten-day supply of jerky and bread and dried apples, plus some cooked rice and beans. You never know when a trip will get longer than you planned.

We checked our bows, made sure the strings weren't worn, then each packed a spare string, just in case.

The last thing my father put in his pack was the scope. "To look back at Lorraine," he said.

The next morning we got up early and ate a big breakfast. When we were finished, my father said, "Well, let's get to it," and we all walked out onto the porch.

The day was beautiful. The volcano was serene. Its ribbon of smoke waved gently as it rose.

My father and I put on our packs and slung our quivers and bows so we could reach them in a hurry if some game tempted us with an easy shot.

My father walked over and kissed Lorraine. "See you in, well, four days, I guess," he said.

I gave Lorraine a kiss, too.

"Have fun," she said. "Take in all the sights."

I felt a tingle of excitement as we stepped off the porch and hitched our loads onto our shoulders.

"Which way, Katie-Bird?" my father asked.

I thought a minute. "It seems to me the crater should always be on our left," I said. "Somehow, it wouldn't feel right to go the other way."

"I agree," Father said. "Would we feel differently if we were left-handed?"

"I can't imagine being left-handed," I said. "It must make everything very hard."

"Left-handers think it's hard being right-handed," he said. "Okay, counterclockwise it is."

We walked up to the edge of the crater and looked down into its vast interior. It would be a long time before today's sun reached every part of its bottom.

"Let's take turns leading," my father said. "I'll start."

We waved to Lorraine. Then we started walking south, my father picking his way among the rocks and shrubs along the crater edge.

We walked in silence. The early-morning sun was bright and warm, and there was just enough breeze to keep us from getting hot.

Obviously, there was no trail, so we made our own. At the start we picked our way over rocks and boulders. Then the rim flattened out, and we hiked through the trees and bushes. As we went farther, some trees seemed to be growing right out of rocks.

It was quiet and beautiful, and suddenly I found myself thinking about the last time I went somewhere new, to Badwater. And Badwater made me think of Adam. He and the sheriff were probably riding through the country somewhere, doing the sheriff's business. I saw Adam sitting ever so erect, looking handsome, smiling and touching his hat to me.

It was a daydream, I guess. I watched as he swung out of his saddle and walked toward me. He was taller than I was. He smiled and took off his hat. He started to say something.

"Careful on these boulders," Father said.

My daydream ended abruptly. We were out of the trees, and a field of boulders lay ahead. Climbing over and around them was going to be hard work, especially after the sun warmed up.

We'd been walking about an hour and a half when my father paused. "Let's take a rest."

We dropped our packs and each picked a smooth rock to

sit on. I unbuttoned the top buttons of my shirt and flapped it in and out, trying to coax some air inside.

We both drank water from our canteens, being careful not to take too much.

After we'd rested awhile, it was my turn to lead.

When you're leading, you see things you don't always see when you're following. It's your job to choose a good path, set a good pace, and keep a sharp eye out for animals or loose stones or any kind of trouble.

We came to a place where the ground turned to rock, smooth and black. There were no trees, no bushes, just wavy black lava hard as granite. A long time ago it had gushed out of the volcano and run down its side. Now it was a black desert where nothing grew.

It wasn't hard to walk on, but you had to be careful where it angled off downhill. Your moccasin might slip, and some places, if you started sliding, it might be a long time before you stopped.

The slanting lava went on for half a mile. We were both happy when we got back to pine trees and plain earth.

My father took over the lead, and I was happy to be a follower again.

When the sun was overhead, Father said, "Let's eat."

We dropped our packs and laid our bows and quivers beside them.

My father said, "I'll go this way." He turned and walked off in the same direction we'd been walking.

"Okay." I walked off back the way we'd come.

This was our routine when we wanted to pee. If the walking was easy and it was a nice day, we might walk far enough to be out of sight of each other. If the walking was hard, with boulders and things, we'd only go a dozen or so steps and just keep our backs turned.

When I finished and turned around, I saw my father walking back fast, frowning. Something was wrong.

I hurried to meet him. As we got closer, I realized he had something in his hand.

"What is it, Father?"

He opened his hand. He was holding the beautiful, round agate Dan Mills had showed us.

FIFTEEN

We stared at it. "What does it mean?" I asked.

My father closed his hand around it. He shook his head. "Nothing good."

"Why would Dan come this way? It's pretty rugged if you're trying to cover distance. Especially if you're an old man."

"Dan's smart," Father said. "If you walk ten or twelve miles around the rim before you start down, it may save you forty or fifty miles on the flat."

"But why would he take out his stone?" I said.

"My guess is, someone took it out for him," my father said. "And I'll bet they took a lot more than that. It looked like there was a struggle."

"Who would steal from an old man?"

Father shook his head. He put the agate into a pocket

deep inside his jacket and looked up at the sun. "We'd better eat," he said. "We may have a long afternoon."

We gnawed on some jerky, ate some cold rice, drank some water. We weren't very hungry.

"I simply can't imagine anyone picking on Dan," I said.

My father just sighed.

When we finished eating, my father looked out over the volcano, then back toward the hillside below. "Put an arrow on your bow," he instructed.

That surprised me. "Do you think there's someone around?" I asked.

"Just being careful."

I hated the thought that we might not be alone. A picture flashed into my mind. A sunny, open field, all by myself. I had just shot a turkey. I turned, and there was Jess.

Well, well, well, it's my old friend the dummy.

I shook my head to clear it. I hated that picture.

As we walked toward where my father had found the marble, I could see the tracks he'd made going out and coming back. We were both twice as alert as we'd been in the morning. We walked silently, watching for any sign of movement.

Our path took us through a thick stand of trees, where we came to a small glade. It was an oval field maybe twenty yards across, grass waving in the breeze. It was very private.

Father stopped and crouched, so I crouched, too. We scanned the field. A bird called, but we saw nothing.

Something moved in the trees on the other side of the glade.

It moved again!

My father stood up. He pulled his arrow to full draw.

A small deer came out from behind a tree. It turned, looked at my father, and dashed off into the forest.

A wave of relief washed over me. It wasn't a man.

Father put his arrow back in his quiver. He took a few steps toward the clearing and motioned me to follow. "I found the agate right here," he said, pointing. "But look at that field, Katie—somebody went crashing right through the middle of it."

We crossed the field, and when we reached the other side, Father pointed at the ground. "Something big happened here."

The grass was trampled, the earth gouged.

"My guess is, someone jumped him," he said. "Two people, probably. I doubt they caught him unawares, he's too cagey for that. But at some point they saw him, and poor Dan was just too old and too slow to get away. This is where they caught him."

He pointed. "Looks like they pulled him into those trees."

We followed a path of flattened grass to another stand of trees. Something heavy had been dragged over the bare earth between the trees. Whoever did it had made no effort to cover their tracks.

My father held up his hand. I stopped.

He stood there, staring. When he turned, his face was ashen.

"Dan?" I said.

He nodded.

I didn't have to ask if he was dead.

"You go back a ways," he told me. "Sit down while I figure out what to do."

"I don't want to go back," I said.

My father looked surprised.

"Whatever it is we have to do, Father, I want to help."

"This is a bad thing, Katie. I don't want you to have to deal with it."

"I have to see him."

"Why?" he asked.

"Because Dan is my friend, too, Father," I said.

I started walking around him.

He blocked the path with his body. "Sorry, Katie."

"I'm not a little girl anymore, Father," I said. "I've depended on you ever since I was born, and I want you to depend on me, too."

"I do depend on you, Katie," he said. "But this is different."

"It's not different," I insisted. "A terrible thing has happened to Dan, and I want to help do whatever it is we have to do."

After a moment, my father stepped off the trail.

"Thank you," I said, and walked past him.

Dan was lying between two big trees. His eyes were open, looking straight up. He had a bloody wound on the side of his head. A handful of flies buzzed around it, and a trail of black ants ran up his neck.

I felt sick.

Our old friend Dan.

I shook my head. I made up my mind not to be sick.

I thought about him sitting at our table having breakfast. I tried to remember how he had looked when I was a little girl. All I could remember were his white buckskins.

And now he was dead.

I thought about the pearls he'd given me. The pearls he'd bought for his own Isabella.

Father walked up and waved the flies away. He knelt and closed Dan's eyes.

"How could anyone do this?" He shook his head in disgust. "What kind of person could attack a sweet old man? It makes my blood boil."

He held the back of his hand against Dan's cheek. "He's pretty cold. My guess is it happened yesterday."

He stood up. "Well, there are some things we have to do, Katie. First, before we walk around too much, let's see what we've got for footprints."

I hadn't even thought about footprints. Now I saw them everywhere.

"One was wearing moccasins!" I said. "Lots of marks on them, too."

"I saw those," he said. "They'll be easy to track. Have you checked the other ones?"

"Boot tracks," I said. "I haven't really looked at them."

My father was silent while I got down on all fours and had a look. I took my time, studying the marks on the soles and heels. Suddenly the boot print spelled itself out for me.

"It's him!" I exclaimed. "It's that person that was with Jess!"

"Good job," he said. "That's his signature, all right. Now, let's take care of Dan."

We looked for his pack. We took our time, but it was nowhere to be seen.

Father knelt and put his hand into the side pocket of Dan's leather jacket. "I feel like a thief," he said.

While he was searching the first pocket, he saw a corner of the leather sack in which Dan kept his treasures. It was mostly under Dan's body. He pulled it out. It was empty. He laid it on the ground and tried a pocket. Empty.

He went through all Dan's pockets. When he had finished, he had a little pile on the ground. An all-purpose cloth, an old comb, some fishhooks wrapped in a scrap of paper. A metal arrowhead, a flat oval rock, smooth, almost polished.

"They didn't leave him much," Father said. "They took everything valuable."

"All his treasures," I said.

My father stood up. "What little they did leave, we'll bury with him."

Bury him? I was puzzled. The ground was baked hard as a rock, and we had nothing to dig with.

"We'll build a cairn," he said. "In the middle of the clearing. We'll cover him with rocks to mark the place where he lies. We'll always know where he is, and it'll keep animals from getting to him."

"A cairn?" I asked.

"It honors the person who's under it. It's a custom from way back."

"We just put rocks right on top of Dan's body?"

"I guess that's how it's done," Father said. "I've never made one."

It didn't seem right to put rocks right on his arms, or his chest, or most of all, on his face. Even if it was an honor, it felt wrong.

"Maybe we could cut some pine branches," I suggested, "and put them over him first. Before the rocks."

My father put his arm around my shoulders. "You're a thoughtful person, Katie. That's a very good idea. Pine branches are soft, and they smell good. Dan would like that."

I thought he might like it, too.

"I've got an idea, too," Father said. "We'll find just the right rocks to make sort of a bridge above his head to protect it. What do you think?"

"Good idea," I said.

"We have to do one other thing first." My father wet Dan's all-purpose cloth with water from his canteen. He washed Dan's face, which didn't have much blood on it, and then the side of his head where he'd been struck.

When he got Dan as clean as he could and straightened his clothing, Father took out his own comb and combed Dan's hair.

"Let's move him to the clearing, and then start getting rocks."

When we'd gathered enough rocks to start, we put the three rocks into place to protect Dan's head. Then we cut a lot of pine boughs. We laid them carefully over Dan's body and arranged them so only the soft ends of the boughs touched him.

Then we put on our first layer of rocks.

We carried and stacked rocks until it was almost too dark to see. After we made camp, we ate a cold supper, drank some water, and climbed into our bedrolls, dead tired.

Just before sunrise, we had a quick breakfast and started again. I looked for big rocks. They seemed to confer more honor than the smaller ones. Of course, we needed the smaller rocks, too, because they filled the spaces between the big ones.

By noon we had a cairn, a big one you would never miss.

"I think we've done it, Katie," Father said.

I wondered what Dan would think of his cairn. I thought he would be glad we built it.

My father stood at the uphill end of the cairn, near Dan's head. He motioned me to come stand beside him. "We should say some words."

He took off his hat, so I took mine off, too.

We were silent for several minutes. Then my father looked at the cairn. "Well, Dan, you've been a good friend to me and my family for a lot of years. And you were a friend to my father before me."

He paused. "You were a fine, brave man. One of the best. An example to all of us. We're grateful to have known you."

My eyes filled with tears, but I didn't cry.

"Some cowards did a terrible thing to you," Father said. "We don't know who they are."

He looked out toward the plain below the volcano. "I'm

going to try to find who did it. That's a promise, old friend. You can count on that."

He sighed. "Katie and I have done the best we can for you, Dan." He paused again. "I guess that's about all I can say."

We stood there, thinking about him and smelling the pine boughs.

I took a deep breath. "My father and I are going to miss you, Dan." A tear ran down my cheek. "Lorraine, too," I said. "We all love you."

I wiped my eyes on my sleeve. "Thanks for the pearls, Dan. They're really beautiful."

After a while we put our hats back on, picked up our packs and our bows and arrows, and started back up to the crater.

SIXTEEN

When we reached the rim, thick clouds of smoke were pouring up from the usual spot in the middle of the volcano, and a second place farther south was smoking, too. I'd never seen smoke come from there before.

"It's angry about Dan," Father said. "Just like us."

Ever since we'd found Dan, neither of us had been hungry. But now our stomachs were complaining, so we ate cold beans and rice and some jerky. I couldn't believe how good it tasted.

While we were eating, my father said, "I want you to go back to the cabin, Katie. I hate sending you alone, but I'm sure you can get there well before dark."

"What are you going to do?" I asked.

"I'm going to track these people," he said. "Looks like they headed south, away from your path back to the cabin. I'm glad of that. The trail's gone pretty cold, but that can't be helped. We had to give Dan a proper burial. But even now I may learn something."

"Like what?"

"I might find something at a campsite. Or I might find some other kind of clue. It's not likely, but I want to try."

"I can go with you, Father. I can be your lookout."

"No." He shook his head. "I want you to go tell Lorraine about Dan. That's important. And tell her what I'm doing. I can't imagine those two are still on the volcano. Once they got Dan's treasures, they were already rich beyond their dreams, so they probably hightailed it. Still, I want to make sure they're actually gone."

"Do you think they were looking for Jess?" I asked.

"Maybe, or maybe looking for us," he said. "Not for you or me actually, but for what we've got."

"The gold," I said, and my father nodded.

Father put his jerky back into his pack. "It's like Lorraine said when we found the glove. I've been trading gold for paper money since before you were born. I guess I've spent too much time trying to convince myself the word hadn't got around, but clearly it has. You know how I tried to fool the sheriff, but I didn't fool him for a minute, and I'm stupid if I think I ever fooled anyone else."

My father stood up, hoisted his pack onto his back.

"You're not stupid, Father."

"Thanks, sweetheart."

"Do you think they know where we live?" I asked.

"No," he said. "They don't know exactly, but someone's trying pretty hard to find out. They didn't come up here to look for Old Dan. He was just a lucky find. No, someone down there wants to find out where that dribble of gold comes from. And they don't want a dribble, they want it all at once."

As I finished loading my pack, I thought about the job of tracking the two brutes who had killed Dan. If anyone could do it, it was my father. He knew everything there is to know about tracking, and about the volcano, and about the land surrounding it. Best of all, he knew how to move without being seen or heard.

I wondered what would happen if he found the killers. He would see them before they saw him, so what would he do? Tie them up and take them to the sheriff? I didn't think so. Too far, too hard.

Would he kill them on the spot?

I didn't think he would do that, either. Maybe I didn't want to know what he would do.

I shouldered my pack.

Father gave me a kiss on the cheek. "Tell Lorraine I'll be back in two days, three at the most." He turned and started walking back down toward the cairn. After a dozen steps he turned around. "Any idea what I'm about to tell you?"

"Hunt as though you're being hunted."

He nodded and went on his way.

SEVENTEEN

I started off toward the cabin. The sun was shining, the air was fresh, it was a perfect day.

I thought about poor Dan, lying under his pine boughs and his rocks. I wondered if it would be disloyal to him if I let myself enjoy the sunshine. No, he would want me to.

Then I thought about "hunting as though I was being hunted," and I put all my thought into checking ahead of me, behind me, down the side of the crater.

I walked nearly an hour without hearing or seeing anything but birds and squirrels. I walked silently without rustling a leaf or stepping on a single twig.

After another hour, I took out my canteen. The water tasted good. I could drink as much as I wanted now, because in a few hours I'd be home.

When I started to screw the top back on, a cold chill ran through my body.

Something had moved.

Downhill.

I scanned the hillside. The near part was covered with grass and brush. Farther down there was a dense curtain of trees.

The rifle scope! But that was in my father's pack, not mine.

Maybe I hadn't seen anything after all.

Maybe my eyes were tired. Maybe I was just tense.

But I didn't think that was true.

Something *had* moved.

It was big.

I took an arrow from my quiver. Not an arrow for birds, but one for deer or wolves. I fitted it to my bow and kept looking.

Could it be a person? My father had said the people who killed Dan would be on their way back to Badwater.

I hoped he was right.

One thing was lucky. Whatever it was, the breeze was blowing from it to me. If it was an animal, it wouldn't be smelling me. If it was a person, well, humans can't smell much anyway.

There was a noise in the trees.

Then I saw it!

A bear! Brown, massive, moving slowly.

I had seen bears many times before, but I had never hunted them. Father said there was too much risk.

He said we could probably bring one down, the two of us, firing arrows as fast as we could, but it might not stay down. Bears were tough and strong, and the bear might just keep on coming, arrows and all.

For a few seconds it seemed as though the bear looked right at me. Then he looked away. He must not have seen me.

He was coming up the hill. Very slowly. He was headed toward the crater's edge, a hundred and fifty yards ahead of me.

I wondered if he was hungry.

Bears are always hungry.

I tried to think what my father would do.

First, he would stay still. He wouldn't make a sound. He wouldn't attract the bear's attention.

I was already doing that. What else would he do?

He would figure out what to do if the breeze shifted. I needed to think about that. He would decide what to do if the bear just plain caught sight of him and saw a delicious dinner.

A blue jay flew down and scolded the bear, then lit in the safety of a nearby pine.

If he saw me, maybe I could climb a tree. I was good at that. I could shed my pack and be up a tree in no time.

But bears were good at climbing, too. Slow, but good. And even if he didn't follow me up the tree, I'd have to stay up there till he went away.

The bear lumbered onward up the hill. He stopped and

shook his head, as though he was trying to shake something out of his ear.

I hadn't moved since I'd first seen him. Without moving my head, I scanned the area around me. I was a few feet from a very big rock that was taller than I was. I wanted to get behind it, but I was afraid to move.

From time to time the bear stopped climbing and looked around, first in my direction, then at the hillside away from me.

The next time he looked away, I wriggled my feet five or six inches toward the big rock, holding my body still.

I stopped, stood stock-still. The bear looked back my way, but he didn't seem to notice anything. The next time he looked away, I did the same thing.

I did it six more times, and on the sixth time I got myself all the way behind the rock.

He couldn't see me now!

I studied the rock. There were some smaller rocks behind it, stunted bushes growing out of its cracks, and a scrubby tree on top. Silently, I stepped onto the smaller rocks and took hold of a bush. I scrambled high enough to peer over the top.

The bear was still climbing. Each step got him closer to cutting me off from my route home.

The breeze shifted ever so slightly. If it shifted a lot, it would reach a point where it was blowing from me to the bear.

Then what?

I thought about weapons. What did the bear have, what did I have?

He had claws, teeth, a tough, heavy body.

I had my bow, arrows, a hunting knife, my canteen, my bedroll, my pack.

Not a great match for a bear.

Inside the pack I had a second canteen, a sweater, food in four leather pouches. One held cooked rice, one beans, one dried fruit, one deer jerky.

I liked deer jerky, so I'd brought a lot. I had a lot left.

The bear reached the edge of the crater. He looked out over it as though he was enjoying the view.

He turned toward my rock, then the other way. He had a decision to make. Which way to go?

If he came toward me, sooner or later he would smell me, smell my jerky, smell good things to eat. No rock would save me then.

If he went the other way? I could probably follow him at a safe distance until he decided to go down the mountain again. Or until a wind shift sent him the delicious smells of me and my jerky.

Jerky. A thought came to me.

I took the leather pouch out of my pack. It was greasy, still two-thirds full.

I looked up. The bear had made his decision. He was lumbering right toward me. He was about a hundred yards away.

Then I got a crazy idea. Strictly out of fear. Out of having to do anything rather than do nothing.

I took some jerky out of the pouch and rubbed it all over my pack—the sides, the top, the bottom, the straps. I rubbed it on the sweater and both canteens.

I stuffed everything back in the pack. Except the jerky bag.

I looked over the rock. My heart beat faster. The bear was fifty yards away. The breeze had picked up.

I rubbed jerky on the outside of its bag to make it as smelly as possible. It didn't need much. It was pretty smelly already.

I put half the meat back in my pack.

Another crazy idea came to me. I pulled the leather thong off the end of my braid and shook out my hair.

The bear was twenty yards away.

Now was the time!

I grabbed the pack and the greasy bag and stood up on the rock.

The wind caught my hair. It streamed out toward the crater.

I shouted as loud as I could. "Ai-yeeee! Ai-yeeee! Ai-yeeee!"

With my arms high, pack in one hand, jerky pouch in the other, I danced up and down on the rock, trying to look fierce. "Ai-yeeee! Ai-yeeee! Ai-yeeee!"

The bear stopped and looked up at me. He looked surprised.

"Ai-yeeee, ai-yeeee!" I whirled in a circle.

I danced. I shouted. I swung my pack around and my hair flew in the wind.

The bear started toward me.

I gave my loudest shout, took aim, and threw the jerky bag at him.

It landed five feet in front of him.

He stopped. He sniffed the pouch.

"Ai-yeeee! Ai-yeeee! Ai-yeeee!"

The bear looked at me, then back at the bag. He nosed it around, picked it up. He chewed. And chewed. And chewed.

Finally, he swallowed.

I whirled my pack around my head. Around and around, in big circles. "Ai-eeee-chaka-chaka!" I screamed. "Ai-eeee-chaka-chaka!"

The pack spun faster and faster. The bear stood still. His head moved slightly as the pack went round and round.

He hadn't met this kind of animal before.

I gave the pack a final desperate whirl and let it fly.

It sailed off, down the steepest part of the hill.

The bear jerked his head, watching. He lifted his head and sniffed.

Which should he go for? The strange animal on the rock? Or the large, smelly bag?

I stood absolutely still.

Time drifted by. Would he never decide?

The bear turned.

He started down the hillside, headed toward the bag.

When he had nearly reached it, I slid off the rock and ran.

I ran as fast as I could, bow in one hand, quiver in the other, hair streaming.

I ran over the uneven ground, across the lava bed, and through the boulder field.

Toward home.

EIGHTEEN

I arrived back at the cabin exhausted, dirty, smelly, hungry, thirsty.

Lorraine was surprised to see me back so soon.

"Katie, what's wrong?" Lorraine said. "Where's your father?"

I told her about Dan, and how two men had attacked and killed him.

I told her my father had gone to track the killers. Even though the trail was cold, he was trying to get an idea of who they might be.

I told her about the bear.

Lorraine hugged me. "Is there anything that hasn't happened to you?" she asked.

My father came back four days later. I cooked a big pheasant dinner to celebrate the three of us being together again.

He'd tracked Dan's killers almost to the base of the volcano.

"I saw good prints of the moccasins," he said. "Long slit running front to back on the left moccasin. And the boots, well, Katie and I know the boots."

"I'm glad you're both home," Lorraine said.

"Me too," my father said. "There's no place on earth like it. But we've got some thinking to do. Dan's being killed means we'd better review our plans for keeping ourselves safe. But let's save that for tomorrow."

Our meeting the next morning didn't take as long as I thought it would. We reviewed our procedures—the signaling and all—and decided not to work the second gun into the system at present. Nobody could think of anything else we could improve. We would just keep on being as careful as we could, always trying to look harder, listen better, and move even more quietly.

It was still early in the day when our meeting ended and we walked out onto our porch. The sun shone, and the volcano sent up a gauzy, broad ribbon of smoke.

"It's a perfect autumn day," Lorraine said. "I wonder how many of these we have left."

My father put one foot up on a bench and leaned on his knee. "Old Dan's talk of winter made me think it's probably a good time to start getting the cabin ready for cold weather. If we get finished early, well, so much the better."

"Good idea, Jack," Lorraine said. "Katie and I will start on the cabin today, and you can take a look to see if the barn and the cool house need any work. We've already brought in lots of wood, but after we're finished with the cabin, maybe Katie and I will get a little more."

It took us two days to get everything ready for cold weather. We washed all the wool blankets, which was a long, heavy job. Then we mended the ones that needed it, which was my least favorite thing to do, and finally we shook and brushed our fur and deerskin robes so we'd all be snug and warm on the coldest nights.

Then it was time to get more wood.

I liked getting wood. It was a friendly job. You didn't talk a lot, but you felt you were a team doing something worthwhile.

Lorraine picked the tree to cut, and we took turns chopping. When we got down to the last few strokes, we paused and looked up.

"Do you want to do it, or shall I?" I asked.

Ever since I was old enough to chop trees with Lorraine, we'd gone through this little routine. I would ask Lorraine if she wanted to make the final chop that would bring the tree down or whether I should do it. And because Lorraine knew how much I liked to do it, she always said, "Why don't you do it, Katie-Bird?"

Now I realized that maybe Lorraine liked it as much as I did.

"You do it this time, Lorraine," I said. "Really. I mean it."

She gave me a great big smile and said, "I wouldn't dream of it."

"No, really," I said.

Lorraine just smiled and pointed to the sideways V on the tree, where we'd been chopping.

Well, just this one more year, I thought. So I looked to see where I wanted my axe to land, and I took an extra-big swing.

The tree took no notice. It stood as steady as ever. I took another giant swing. Same result. On my third swing the tree shuddered.

After the next swing, we heard a small cracking sound. I stepped back. The cracking got louder. Then it became big, loud, serious, and the tree began to fall. Slowly, slowly, faster, then with a rush. As it crashed to the ground, the butt jumped backward over the stump.

"Good job," Lorraine said.

"Teamwork," I said.

We stripped off the limbs, then picked up the two-man saw and went to work on the trunk. One of us pulled the saw one way, the other pulled it back. Back and forth, back and forth.

"Look at us," Lorraine said. "Two women sawing up a tree, and they call it a two-man saw!"

One night about a week later, after we'd finished dinner, my father said, "I've got something to tell you, Katie-Bird."

This was odd. Usually my father didn't tell me he was going to tell me something. He just told me.

"You know how Lorraine sometimes leaves us to go out

and make her medical rounds?" he said. "And it may be a month or whatever before she comes back?"

"You haven't done that so much lately, Lorraine," I said. "I'm glad."

"I'm older," she explained. "A new woman's been helping me out this last year, and now she's going to take over."

"So," Father continued, "from now on she's not going to go off on those trips at all. She's going to live here full time. I talked her into it."

"That's really great, Lorraine!"

"It's the other way around," Lorraine said. "I talked your father into it."

Father leaned back in his chair and smiled. "There's even more, Katie. Lorraine has agreed to marry me."

"Oh, Lorraine!" I went over and gave her a hug and a kiss.

"You know, Katie," Father said, "when I married your mother in Little Fish, a preacher married us. But Lorraine and I don't need a preacher. We love each other, and that's what matters, so we're going to get married right out there on the edge of the crater. And we'd like you to be our special attendant."

"Nothing would make me happier," I said.

They got married the next afternoon.

In the morning Lorraine and I went down to the washing pond and bathed and helped each other wash our hair. About mid-afternoon we all put on our best clothes. Lorraine wore a long, silky green dress. I didn't even know she had a dress.

With her dark reddish hair streaming down over her shoulders, she looked beautiful. My father wore a dark blue cloth coat, with pants that matched. I'd never seen them before, either. He also wore a white shirt, open at the collar. He looked good.

As I looked at the two of them, it seemed they had both become ten or fifteen years younger.

I wore my buckskin skirt, which still looked quite new, and a white shirt. That was as dressed up as I could get.

Then I remembered Dan's pearls. I got them out of their little leather pouch and Lorraine helped me put them on.

At five o'clock the three of us walked out to the rim of the volcano. The sun was still shining, the volcano was smoking idly, and the shadow had barely started up the other side of the crater.

My father and Lorraine faced each other with miles and miles of volcano behind them. They held each other's hands and looked into each other's eyes. My father was the first to speak.

"I want the whole world to know," he said, "that I love Lorraine more than I can say, and I don't ever want to be separated from her. Even though she's very good at taking care of herself, I want her to be my wife, so I can take care of her for the rest of my life."

Then it was Lorraine's turn.

"I want the whole world to know," she said, "that I love Jack MacDonald, and I always will. I don't ever want to be separated from him, or from our wonderful Katie, who is my best friend after Jack, or from our wonderful home on the edge of the volcano."

Happy tears ran down my cheeks.

My father turned to me. "And now," he said, "would you pronounce us husband and wife?"

I stepped up close. They were still holding hands. I looked at Lorraine, then I looked at my father.

"I pronounce you husband and wife," I said.

My father took Lorraine in his arms and kissed her, and then they each opened one arm to me, and I moved in close so we could all put our arms around one another. It was the best day of my life.

NINETEEN

Life didn't change much after Lorraine and my father got married, and that was good. We went about the jobs we had to do, just as we always had. We made Billy and Valerie haul even more wood, and then we made them haul water from the spring in the heavy waxed canvas sacks Lorraine had made. We dumped it into the covered wooden boxes that were our water supply winter and summer.

One thing was different, though. Our cabin had always been a happy place, but now it was happier than ever. My father and Lorraine made me feel as though something wonderful was happening every day.

I wondered how that all came about. The only difference in our lives was that Father and Lorraine had stood on the rim of the crater and said some words to each other. Otherwise, everything was the same. Still, there was something new going on in our cabin, something that helped me think less about some of the bad things that had happened, about Jess, and about losing Dan. Did saying those words have the power to change our lives that much?

I found myself thinking a lot about Adam Summerfield. I'd barely met him, the two of us sitting on our horses like mutes while the sheriff talked to my father. I'd seen him and heard him say his name, that was all.

But in a funny way I felt he was a good man. Maybe a very good man.

Then I told myself: Stop being so silly! You don't know him at all!

But deep inside, I thought I did.

Autumn was making its usual changes. The mornings were cooler, and the leaves had turned red and yellow. But it was still hot at midday, almost like summer.

One afternoon, two or three weeks after the wedding, we were all sitting out on the porch resting between jobs when my father suddenly sat up very straight. "Shhh!"

He cupped one ear with his hand. Lorraine and I sat up, too. We all listened hard.

"I hear it," Lorraine said.

"Me too," I whispered. I ran to get my bow.

My father went inside, got the gun from its hiding place, and slipped it inside his jacket. Lorraine and I strung our bows, then went back to the porch and laid everything on the floor beside the benches. We all sat down again.

Ten minutes later a horseman came around the edge of the trees on our left, up near the crater. He was about fifty yards away when we first saw him. A minute later a second horseman appeared.

Father squinted at the pair. "Why, that's the sheriff," he said. "Well, I'll be darned!"

The riders got closer.

We all stood up and my father walked out to meet them. "Hello, Sheriff," he said. "Sheriff Benson, isn't it? Welcome to Tenspike."

The sheriff's eyebrows shot up. "I thought Tenspike was out on the flat, couple of days' ride south of Badwater."

Father smiled. "Don't know who ever gave you that idea."

The sheriff laughed and swung down from his horse. "Mr. MacDonald. How are you?"

They shook hands.

"We had a time finding you," the sheriff said. "I was pretty sure you lived up here somewhere, but it's a mighty big volcano. Just got lucky, I guess."

The sheriff's deputy rode up, sitting very erect. He touched his hat to my father. "Mr. MacDonald."

He looked over to us on the porch, smiled, and touched his hat again.

I couldn't believe it was Adam! But of course it was. I waved back, astonished that my arm actually worked. I'd thought a lot about Adam, but in reality I wasn't sure I'd ever see him again. Much less at our cabin!

My father and the sheriff came to the edge of the porch. I stood up.

The sheriff looked at me. "This is George, I believe," he said. "Do I have that right?"

"Once upon a time this was George," Father said. "But as I'm sure you remember, we call her Katie now. Katie, you remember the sheriff."

"Good afternoon, Sheriff." I went to the edge of the porch and shook hands.

My father motioned toward Lorraine. "This is Mrs. Mac-Donald. Lorraine, Sheriff Benson."

"Hello, Sheriff," she said.

The sheriff took off his hat, stepped onto the porch, and shook hands with Lorraine.

He looked at our cabin. "This must be Tenspike Town Hall."

Father laughed. "You've got us pretty well figured out, Sheriff. Now, you must be hot from your ride. Hungry, too, I expect. Come on in and let's fix that. Your deputy, too. What's his name?"

"Adam," I said.

Everyone looked at me. My face got hot.

"Summerfield," Sheriff Benson said. "Adam Summerfield."

"Katie," Lorraine said, "why don't you show Deputy Summerfield where he can water the horses. Then bring him back up here."

"Sure," I said.

The others went inside. Outside, Deputy Summerfield still sat on his horse. I walked over and held my hand up to him.

"I'm Katie," I said.

He leaned down from the saddle and shook my hand. "I remember. I'm Adam."

I figured what he remembered was a dirty-faced kid who'd been banged up in a fight.

"I remember, too," I said. "Come on, we'll water your horses."

I took the reins of the sheriff's horse and led him down toward the barn. Adam got off his horse and followed.

"You live in a great place," Adam said. "It must be a real treat to wake up every morning and look out and see that huge crater."

"It is," I said.

I wanted to say something nice about where he lived, too. That was the polite thing to do. But he lived in Badwater— the opposite of a nice place.

"How long have you lived here?" he asked.

"I was born here," I said.

"Wow," he said, patting his horse's neck.

I couldn't think of anything to say, I was so nervous. But Adam's horse saved me. He whinnied. He was a beautiful animal.

"I like your horse," I said.

What I was really thinking was, I liked the look of Adam Summerfield.

We watered the horses at an outside trough, then brought them into the barn. Billy and Valerie nickered as Adam unsaddled the sheriff's horse, then his own. He took a cloth out of one saddlebag and gave the sheriff's horse a rubdown, especially where the saddle had been. I got one of our cloths and did the same for his horse.

"You must have had a long ride today," I said. "All uphill, too."

"We walked a good bit of it," Adam said. "This volcano is kind of tough on horses."

I liked that he took such good care of his horse. I guessed the sheriff was the same.

"I always wondered what it would be like to look down into this volcano," he said. "Does it always smoke?"

"Yes," I said, "but it's got a lot of different ways of doing it."

When we finished with the horses, we went up to the cabin. My father and Lorraine and the sheriff were sitting at the big table. The two chairs from the bedrooms had been brought out. The sheriff had a plate of cold pheasant in front of him and was drinking from a big glass of water.

Lorraine had set a place for Adam.

"Have a seat, Mr. Summerfield," she said. "You've had a long day."

"Thank you, ma'am," Adam said.

He sat down, and I sat down across from him. He drank half his glass of water, then started on the pheasant.

"So, Sheriff," my father said, "what brings you up to this part of the world?"

"Well, not too long ago two young fellows from town told their friends they were going hunting up on the volcano."

"Hunting's pretty good up here this time of year," my father agreed.

"Problem is, one of the young fellows never came back," Sheriff Benson said.

Nobody said anything.

"His hunting partner came back," he continued, "came back early, in fact. The other fellow's horse came back, too, but not the fellow himself. Tall fellow, on the heavy side, dark hair. You haven't seen anyone like that, have you?"

"Sheriff, you're the first person we've seen since Katie and I got back from Badwater," my father told him.

"Any idea what could have happened to a fellow like that?" the sheriff asked.

"No idea," Father answered.

"Thought it might have been a hunting accident," the sheriff said, "but his rifle was in his scabbard. Hadn't been fired."

"So I guess he hadn't been hunting after all," my father said.

"He had a pistol, too," the sheriff said. "I guess he was wearing that."

"Makes sense," my father said.

"We backtracked the horses," Sheriff Benson explained, "and we found where they camped, up north of here, about three-quarters of the way to the crater. The first fellow went back after one night. We wanted to follow the other fellow's footprints away from there, but I guess you had some rain or something, because they were all washed out."

"So you're here to search for him," Father said. "If you want to stay here while you go about your work, we'd be glad to have you."

The sheriff looked thoughtful. "That's mighty nice of you. We might just do that."

"You can sleep in my room, Sheriff," I offered. "I'll sleep out here."

"Thank you, Katie," the sheriff said, "but Deputy Summerfield and I will sleep outside. Maybe on your porch, if that's all right with Mr. MacDonald."

"Wherever you'd like, Sheriff," my father said.

"If we could come back here at the end of the day, that would be a treat to look forward to."

"Good," Lorraine said. "It's nice to have company."

After I was in bed, I thought about Adam, of course, but I also thought of having two lawmen staying with us. We knew what had happened to the person they were looking for, so I suppose we should've all felt nervous. My father and Lorraine didn't seem to feel that way, and I didn't either.

The only thing I felt nervous about was Adam.

Now that I'd seen him again, I found myself wondering: Does he like me? Does he think I'm pretty?

TWENTY

Lorraine was right. It was nice to have company.

When it was just the three of us, we ate at one end of the big table, the one nearest the fire. Whatever we were working on at the time—a new axe handle, a pair of moccasins— was left sitting on the other end. But with guests for dinner, Lorraine and I cleared the whole table and gave it a good scrubbing.

Lorraine roasted venison. I knew Adam and the sheriff would love it. When we sat down to eat, though, it felt strange. With five chairs around the table, and five people eating and talking, the cabin seemed a whole lot smaller.

Adam and I didn't talk much, because Sheriff Benson and my father and Lorraine all had so much to say. It almost seemed as though there were two different groups at the table. The three older people belonged to one very talkative group, while Adam and I were a small, quiet group of our own. We just listened, and looked at each other now and then, and smiled.

It was interesting to hear what the sheriff had to say. He told stories about the rougher days of Badwater, about tracking down burglars and thieves and murderers. He wasn't bragging, he was just telling what had happened.

He told us how he'd tracked people and caught them, and also how sometimes he'd tracked people for many days and nights, and they got away anyhow.

And he told us how Badwater had actually become much safer. He said, thanks to New Pacifica being calmer compared to the old days, Badwater was calmer, too. New families coming had made a big difference, and people seemed to be more interested in setting up new businesses than in shooting each other.

The sheriff asked lots of questions, too. He wondered what it was like to live so far from a town, with no neighbors. He wanted to know where we got our water, and what we ate in the winter, and what we did to amuse ourselves when we were snowed in.

Father and Lorraine answered most of his questions, but I answered the one about how we amused ourselves in the winter. I told him about my mother's books and how my father and I had read them all many times.

"What books did she have?" he asked.

"Well, I'm reading *Pilgrim's Progress* right now," I said, "for about the tenth time, but we've also got *Vanity Fair*, and *A Tale of*

Two Cities, and a book about King Arthur, and *Frankenstein*—I really like *Frankenstein.* And *Pride and Prejudice,* and half a dozen others. They're all good."

"I like to reread books," the sheriff said. "I've got some books I never get tired of. Every time I read them, I find something new."

"Do you ever take a book along to read when you're out searching?" I asked.

The sheriff smiled. "No, Katie. By the end of the day, Deputy Summerfield and I are ready to cook some grub and spread our bedrolls. If I had a book along, I'd use it as a pillow."

I was sorry he didn't have a book with him, because it would have been interesting to see what it was about. But then I thought, having new people around was ever so much better than seeing a new book.

The sheriff and Adam were up early the next morning. They ate deer jerky and dried apples for breakfast, then saddled up. They said they were going to ride north. One of them would cover the area just below the crater edge, and the other would ride the same direction, only lower down. Coming back, they'd ride lower still, to cover new ground and thereby search as much of the volcano as they could.

"I want to warn you about one thing," my father told them. "There's a big split in the earth about a mile north of here. Runs downhill from the crater for, I don't know, half a mile. It's deep. You wouldn't want to stumble on it unawares."

"Thanks," the sheriff said, "we'll look out for that."

We watched till they were out of sight, then went indoors.

"It's a strange, strange world we live in," Father said. "They're looking for something we know they can't find, and we're helping them not find it."

We spent the day just like any other day. Lorraine and I went bird hunting to the south, to stay clear of the searchers. We headed toward one of our favorite little meadows. It was carved abruptly out of the side of the volcano and was grassy and flat for maybe two hundred yards before it ran downhill again.

"How do you like the sheriff?" Lorraine asked.

"He's nice," I said. "I met him in town."

"I know," she said. "What do you think of his man Friday?"

"His what?" I knew what she meant, because *Robinson Crusoe* is one of my mother's other books. I just wanted time to think what to say.

"His deputy. What's his name?"

"Adam." I looked at Lorraine. She was smiling, and I knew she was teasing me.

"I like him," I said. "Don't you?"

"Oh, yes." Lorraine grinned. "I like him. He's pretty quiet, though, isn't he?"

"Well, the sheriff does most of the talking," I said. "But Adam is nice, and he's very polite, and I think he's a gentle kind of person. Of course, I haven't really seen him that much."

"What do you think of his looks?" Lorraine asked, raising her eyebrows.

"I like his looks a lot, Lorraine," I admitted. I could feel my face getting red. "But you know that already. You know every-thing that goes on in my head."

"I like his looks, too," she said.

We set up at the downwind end of the meadow. Lorraine took one side, just out of sight in the trees, and I took the other. We both had a wide field for shooting, without any danger of shooting each other.

It was a long day, but a good one. It took five hours, but we came home with three pheasants, four partridges, and a turkey.

Lorraine and I plucked and fixed the birds together. When we were through, she turned to me, looking thoughtful.

"I think we should wear our skirts tonight," she said.

"Okay," I agreed.

"And you should undo your braid and comb your hair out. I'll help you."

"You do it, too, Lorraine," I said. "We'll both do it."

"No." She shook her head. "Just you."

After we'd cleaned up dinner that night, Adam and I sat out on the porch and talked. We asked the others if they wanted to come out, too, but they said it was too cool.

It wasn't too cool. They just thought it would be nice to let the young people talk to each other without adults around. And it was.

For a while we just sat there and looked at the crater. It wasn't dark yet, just dusky. Way out in the middle you could still see the smoke rising. Closer, a bunch of barn swallows were wheeling and diving right in front of us, catching the last insects.

"It's amazing you were born right here," Adam said.

"I can't imagine what it would be like to be born somewhere else," I said. "Where were you born? Badwater?"

"I was born in the mountains on the other side," he said. "Grew up there. I just came down to Badwater looking for work."

"And you went to work for the sheriff?" I said.

"No," he said. "I got a job digging holes. I'm a great hole digger."

"Who did you dig holes for?"

"The cemetery in town," he said.

"You're a grave digger!" I said.

Adam laughed. "I *was* a grave digger, but now I've come up in the world. At least it feels like it, following the sheriff around and wearing a star."

I'd never had an experience like this one. Just sitting and talking with someone near my age. It was completely different from talking with my father or Lorraine.

In some of my books I'd read about young men and young women meeting and talking. Usually they talked very formally, and sometimes they said things they didn't really mean. They were trying to impress the other person. Or maybe they wanted to get something from them. Many times, if they were young women, they were trying to get the young man to marry them.

I wondered what it would be like to be married. My father

and Lorraine were married, but that was somehow different. They were older, they'd known each other for years and years. That was a lot different from me and Adam.

I wondered what it would be like to be married to Adam. I wondered if we could ever become the kind of partners who would do something really courageous, like pulling up stakes and moving off into the unknown, the way my parents had.

I decided we could. Adam looked like the kind of person who wasn't afraid of things and could face up to hard situations.

"How old are you?" I said.

Adam laughed. "Nineteen."

"Why did you laugh?" I asked.

"Most people don't just come out and ask you like that."

"How else could I find out how old you are?"

"Well, I don't know," he said. "It's a perfectly decent question. How old are you?"

"Sixteen," I said. "Sixteen and a half, really."

"If we're going to get into fractions," he said, "I'm actually nineteen and three-quarters."

"How long have you worked for the sheriff?"

He thought a minute. "One year, nine months."

"Do you like it?" I said.

"Sheriff Benson's a great guy. Yeah, I like working for him."

"Beats digging holes?" I asked.

Adam laughed. "Sure does. How about you? What do you do up here all the time?"

"Well, we spend a lot of time making sure we have food," I

said. "You know, hunting birds or deer, looking for nuts, mushrooms, berries. We even raise a few vegetables."

"Are you always going to live here?" he asked.

"Where else would I live?"

Adam considered. "Well, you could live in a town."

"Like Badwater?" I said.

"No, no, not like Badwater." He shook his head. "Some other kind of town. Of course, since I've never seen another town, that's not much of a recommendation. Maybe you could live on some other mountain."

"But why?" I asked, looking out over the volcano. "Why would I want to move?"

"I don't know," Adam said. "If I lived here, I don't think I'd want to move either."

For a while we sat quietly, watching the crater grow dimmer. Then Adam broke the silence. "You have really beautiful hair."

A warm feeling ran through my body. I couldn't remember feeling anything like it before. Lorraine said things like that from time to time, but it didn't make me feel this way.

"Thank you," I said.

I tried to think of something to say back.

"You and I," I said, "we've both got about the same color hair."

"But yours is nice the way it flows down over your shoulders," he said, "and down your back."

We didn't say a whole lot after that. We hadn't said much, but I had a feeling that something significant had happened.

As we sat there, saying nothing, it felt very comfortable and warm.

The next morning the sheriff and Adam went off to search south. My father told them the crater rim was rockier to the south and might be hard going for their horses.

The sheriff thanked him and asked if they might leave their horses with us.

"Of course," Father said.

The sheriff set out in the lead. I watched them go. Just before they rounded the trees at the start of the boulder field, Adam turned and waved.

I waved back with a big sweep of my arm.

All day long Father and I worked down at the cool house. My father had built it right over where the spring came out of the ground. The spring ran cold, and that kept the inside of the little building nice and chilly, even on the hottest days. We hung venison here, and birds, and other game.

We renewed some of the supports inside the cool house so that when cold weather came, we could stand on them and chip at the ice that formed around the spring. If we kept the ice free, the spring kept running.

Lorraine spent her day working on a new warm jacket for my father. She was making it from the pelts of some wolves that had been trying to get into the barn and cool house the previous winter.

We were all good and tired by the time the sheriff and Adam came back. We brought the two bedroom chairs out onto the porch, and all sat there drinking cold water flavored with wild mint.

"So how'd it go?" my father asked.

"We found a cairn," Sheriff Benson said. "Quite new. Know anything about it?"

TWENTY-ONE

Katie and I built it, " my father said.

"So who's under it?" the sheriff asked.

"Our old friend Dan Mills, eighty-three, and tough as they come."

"How'd he die, and how'd you happen to bury him way out there?"

"Couple of people killed him with a rock," Father told him. "Knocked him on the head, took his money and what he called his treasures. Stuff he'd collected over the years, some of it quite valuable. Gold, carved ivory, trinkets."

"How do you know all this?" the sheriff asked.

"He stayed with us this autumn," my father said. "He left to go to a warmer climate for the winter. Took off early. Didn't want to deal with snow anymore."

"And how is it you know it was two men that killed your friend?" Sheriff Benson asked.

"After Dan left us, Katie and I decided to hike all the way around the crater. Halfway into our first day we came on Dan's body. You could see there'd been a fight. We found footprints—a pair of moccasins and a pair of boots. Katie and I built the cairn, and then I tracked the prints as far as I could."

"Find anything?"

"A campsite," Father said. "More prints. I could identify those moccasins, and those boots, too, if I ever saw them again."

"I see," the sheriff said. "So if Summerfield and I spend tomorrow taking that cairn apart, stone by stone, when we get to the bottom, we'll find an old man. Is that what you're saying?"

"That's right," Father answered. "And if you feel you have to do it, we'll help you."

"I haven't said we're going to do it yet," the sheriff said. "But didn't you tell me that Summerfield and I were the first people you'd seen since you got back from Badwater?"

"Dan's more like family, so I forgot to mention him," my father said. "I'm sorry."

Sheriff Benson made an entry in a notebook. "Now, about the man we're looking for. You're sure you didn't see him? Don't know anything about him at all?"

"Afraid I can't help, Sheriff," Father said.

"That's not quite answering my question," the sheriff said.

"What I'd like are a couple of yes or no answers. One, did you see him, and two, do you know anything about him?"

"No on both questions."

After dinner that night Adam and I sat out on the dark porch again. I thought back to how nervous I was the first time we talked. That was all gone.

"We're going back tomorrow," Adam told me.

"I think you should search some more," I said.

"So do I," he said. "It seems like we just got here. But the sheriff thinks we've done what we came to do. So that's it. We're going."

I hated the idea that Adam had to go. I wanted more dinners with him around the big table. I wanted more evenings with him out on the porch in the gathering darkness. Now that he was going, I realized how seriously I was going to miss him.

"Will you come up here again?" I asked.

"I'd really like it if we did," Adam said. "But it depends on the sheriff. Where he goes, I go. At least for the present."

"Oh."

"But if he ever gives me any time off, I'll be back," Adam said. "I haven't had any time off since I started, though. I don't think he believes in it."

He paused. "But I will get up here, Katie. I really do want to see you again." He put his hands on top of mine and held them there. "One way or another, sheriff or no sheriff, I'll be back. That's a promise."

We just sat there, together on the bench. It was quiet and beautiful in the darkness. After a while I felt his hand stroking my hair. I moved closer and put my head on his shoulder. He put his arm around me. I felt a wonderful little shiver run through my body, a kind of shiver I didn't want to end. We sat there for a long time, neither of us saying a word.

We all had an early breakfast together the next morning. After we finished, the sheriff leaned back in his chair and looked my father in the eye.

"One more thing, Jack," he said. "I call you Jack because I think you're a good man, someone I'd like to have as a friend. But I'm puzzled, Jack."

"Why's that, Sheriff?"

"My name's Fred," the sheriff said. "If you're Jack, I'm Fred. Here's what puzzles me. I understand why you said you came from Tenspike, and told me Katie was a boy, and all that. I knew those things weren't true the minute you said them."

"I know you did, Fred," my father admitted.

"I don't hold it against you. You were protecting your home and your daughter. But we've got a different situation here now, Jack, and I think you know more than you're letting on."

The room went silent.

"Now, you may have a good reason why you're holding back," the sheriff said. "And I do hope it's good, and concerned with everyone's safety and all that. But I know you know something, Jack. And I'm not going to ask you any more, because I know you're not going to tell me."

The room was still quiet.

"So all there is to do now," Sheriff Benson said, getting to his feet, "is thank you all for your hospitality. It's been a pleasure to know that when we finished our day's work, we'd be coming back here to you nice people."

"We've enjoyed it, too," Father said.

"I believe Deputy Summerfield shares my opinion," the sheriff added.

Adam straightened up, surprised. "Yes, sir," he said. He stood up and looked at my father, then at Lorraine, then at me. "I do indeed share that opinion. It's been a great pleasure to be here with you. It really has, and I thank you. All of you."

TWENTY-TWO

The next few days felt very empty. It had been wonderful having Adam to talk to, and to stroke my hair in the dark. I missed hearing his voice, looking into those brown eyes.

Adam had promised he would come back. A promise was a very important thing to me. In some of my mother's books, though, people sometimes made promises they didn't keep. But these were generally characters I didn't like, and I liked Adam a lot.

He would keep his promise.

The morning after Adam and the sheriff left, we had snow.

By noon, however, the sun was shining hot as ever, and the snow was gone. But we'd had our warning. It seemed as though autumn had barely started, yet here was winter, telling us it could move in anytime it felt like it.

Then one day in late autumn, while Lorraine and I were

cutting up buckskin to make gloves, my father came running into the cabin. He'd been out hunting birds, but he was back early because something was wrong.

"Armed man on horseback," he said. He went to the box near the front door, picked up the gun, and slid it inside his jacket.

I had a quick thought.

Adam?

But my father wouldn't look concerned if it were Adam. He turned to Lorraine. "Get the extra gun, but don't let him see it," he said.

I strung my bow and laid it on the floor of the porch, along with my quiver of arrows. We all sat down on the benches. My father's bow, arrows, and game bag were lying at his feet.

The horseman came from the north, the same way the sheriff and Adam had come. He was riding a nice-looking chestnut mare, and he headed straight for the cabin. The mare carried saddlebags on both sides, and the rider had a scabbard with a rifle under his right leg.

He was about my father's age, I guessed, on the fat side, with a yellowy face. His gun belt was filled with bullets, and his holster held a revolver.

He came closer. He didn't speak, he didn't raise his hand, he didn't touch his hat.

My father stepped off the porch and walked up to him. "Good morning." He looked up at the sun. "I guess it's still morning. I'm Jack MacDonald."

He held his hand up to shake, but the horseman didn't accept the offer. Father lowered his hand.

The man looked around at the crater, the trees, and at our cabin. His face was grim. "I made the sheriff tell me where to find you," he said. He looked from my father to the bench where Lorraine and I sat.

"What can we do for you?" Father asked him.

"I'm looking for my son," he said.

"And who is your son?"

"You know damn well who my son is," the man said. "The sheriff was up here talking to you about him a few weeks ago."

"Sheriff Benson, yes," my father said. "I'm sorry to say we couldn't help him much, and I doubt we're going to be much help to you. We told the sheriff everything we knew, which was basically nothing. We live up here all by ourselves, hardly see a soul from one year's end to the next."

"I know all about that," the man said gruffly. "I read that fool sheriff's report. He stayed with you, didn't he."

It sounded like an accusation.

"He and his deputy were with us several days," Father told him. "They searched two days, and came back here both nights."

"Not much of a search, I'd say."

"Seemed to me they worked pretty hard."

"Seems to me you worked pretty hard on them!" the man spat out. "Report says they found a big cairn south of here, but you sweet-talked them into not opening it."

"I told the sheriff who's under that cairn," my father said

calmly, "and I told him my daughter and I put him there after he'd been murdered by thieves. He was an old friend, eighty-three years old. I tracked his killers as best I could, but I came up dry. And that's the truth, and that's what I told the sheriff. And yes, he believed me, because he could see it was true."

"How could he see that?" the man asked.

"You'll have to ask him," my father said.

"I'm not asking him, I'm asking you. How could he know for sure who's under that cairn without taking it apart?"

"Well, sir," my father replied, "I'm very sorry your son is lost. I respect you for coming up here to look for him."

The man's face didn't change.

"That being said, sir," my father continued, "I hope you will respect me when I tell you the man underneath all those rocks is definitely not your son."

"Don't 'sir' me," the man said. "I know my son's up here somewhere, alive or dead. There's a body under those rocks, maybe not just one body. That stupid sheriff didn't even look. His report says at first he thought it might have been my boy. But then he talked to you, and you spun him some story about your dear old lifelong friend, and how he's under those rocks. Well, sirrrrr, I don't buy a word of it."

Father stood still for a long time, looking up at the man in the saddle. "Well, it's the truth," he said at last. Then he came back onto the porch.

The man glared at my father. "Maybe that sheriff ain't got the sense to look under that cairn, but I damn well have!"

He looked around as though he was not quite sure what

to do next. He clucked to the mare and started to ride off to the south. Then he turned around and rode back to where we sat.

"That cairn," he said, "off to the south, is it?"

My father pointed to our right. "You go around those trees, then just follow the curve of the volcano. You'll come to a big patch of black lava, runs for nearly half a mile. Very soon after that you'll see a big oak, standing alone, almost at the volcano rim. Look downhill from there, down to the right, and you'll see a grove of aspens. You walk through, and in the middle you'll find a meadow. That's the place. About a half day's walk."

The man was silent, didn't move.

"It'll be pretty rough going for your mare," my father said. "Boulders, lava field, so on. If you want to leave her here, we'll look after her."

"I've already lost a son. I ain't about to lose a horse."

Father sat back down in his chair. "Just an idea."

The man rode off toward the stand of trees.

We all just sat there.

"He's got a right to be unhappy," my father said. He got up and went into the cabin.

TWENTY-THREE

Lorraine put the extra gun back in the bureau she shared with Father, and she and I went back to cutting up buckskin. It was hard to keep my mind on it after the angry outbursts from Jess's father. I was not used to people showing anger. I didn't like it, but I knew he had reason.

My father sat, staring out the cabin door. Outside, the volcano was sending up a thicker stream of smoke than usual.

"What do you think he'll do, Jack?" Lorraine asked. "Tear down the cairn?"

"First he'll find out his mare can't handle the boulders," he said. "Then he's got a decision. Should he hobble the mare and leave her there while he goes exploring, or should he come back here and eat crow? He doesn't want to do either one. He doesn't want to ask us to take care of her, because, one, he doesn't trust us, and two, he thinks I killed his son."

He paused. "Which, unfortunately, I did."

"Oh, Jack." Lorraine sighed.

"He doesn't know the circumstances," Father said. "But even if he did, it wouldn't matter. I can understand that. Right or wrong, it's his son."

He was silent for a moment. "I might feel the same way if I were in his shoes."

Lorraine walked over and put her hands on his shoulders. She leaned over and pressed her face against his.

"You're a good man, Jack," she said. "Don't forget that."

He turned his head and kissed Lorraine's cheek.

"You'll figure out what to do," she said. "You always do."

"Well, one way or another, he's got to come back here," my father said. "Maybe tonight, maybe in the morning. My guess is he'll leave the mare with us, then go find the cairn so he can decide whether he's going to take it down or not."

"I hope he decides not to," I said.

"It won't be an easy job," he said. "You and I laid stones for a day and a half. It's not going to be easy for one man, living on dry rations and not much water."

Father put his gun back in the box near the front door.

"Well, at least he's not an outlaw after our gold," he said.

About sundown the man appeared again. He rode up to the cabin slowly. My father stood out on the porch, waiting.

"Maybe I spoke too hasty," the man said. "Like you said, that's a rough patch of ground. Maybe I should have taken your offer to keep my horse."

"Offer's still open," Father said.

"Maybe I could get some water from you," the man said. "I've let myself get a little short."

"All the water you want," Father said. "Food, too, if you want to join us. We're about to eat."

"Just the water. And the horse. I've got my own rations."

"I'll get you the water. Katie'll put your mare in the barn and see she gets fed." My father took the canteen to fill it.

"I want a couple of things off her before she goes," the man said to me, taking his bedroll and a pack off the horse.

He pulled his rifle from his saddle scabbard. "And I guess I'll take this." He laid it against his bedroll.

My father came out of the cabin and handed him the filled canteen. The man started off toward the trees.

I led the mare down the path to the barn.

As I put her in a stall and fed her, I kept thinking about Jess. The son this man was searching for and would never find. My father and Lorraine had both told me, more than once, that I had no responsibility for his death. None whatsoever. I knew it was true. All I had done was react when he attacked me, first in Badwater, then on the volcano.

Then I remembered what he'd looked like in life, even though he'd been nasty, and how young he'd been, and thought of him lying there at the bottom of The Crease, the bottomless pit, his life over forever. I almost started to cry.

At lunch the next day my father said, "I've been thinking about the man out at the cairn."

"Me too," I said.

"He's gotten there about now," Father said, "if he's found it at all, and he's looking at an enormous pile of rocks."

He paused, thinking. "He's absolutely sure his son's under there. We know he isn't, but he'll go to his grave thinking his son's there until he sees it with his own two eyes."

"You're right, Jack," Lorraine said.

"So I'm going to help him," my father said.

"How?" Lorraine asked.

"I'm going to pack up some food and water, and I'm going out there and help him prove his son isn't there. Then I'll start putting those rocks back on Old Dan."

"I'll help you, Father," I said.

"Let me go with your father, Katie-Bird," Lorraine said. "You stay and look out for the horses."

Lorraine was trying to spare me having to look at Dan's body again. A lot would have changed since we put him there.

"Thanks, Lorraine," I said, "but I want to go. I was there to help build the cairn, and if it's got to come down, then I want to be part of putting it back up again."

"I understand, sweetheart," she said. "Of course you should go."

TWENTY-FOUR

It took us a little over an hour to get our packs ready, and it was close to mid-afternoon when we set out. We figured we'd get halfway there by sundown and camp.

We got up early the next morning, had a quick breakfast, and a few hours later we walked through broken sunlight into the grove of trees that surrounded Dan's meadow. When we stepped into the clearing, we expected to see the man pulling stones from Dan's cairn.

But no one was there. The cairn was untouched.

My father put his hands on either side of his mouth and shouted, "Hello!"

He turned in each direction and shouted again, very loud, "Hello!"

The only sound was the breeze.

"Looks like he overshot," Father said.

We stood for a minute, thinking.

"Best thing to do, I guess," he said, "is to keep going along the rim and keep shouting."

We went back up to the rim and headed south again, shouting "hello" as we went. We found Jess's father a half mile farther along. He was sitting on a rock, drinking from his canteen. I had the feeling he'd heard some of our hellos but hadn't answered. He didn't say a word as we walked up.

"The cairn's back a ways," my father said.

"Damn poor set of directions," the man replied.

My father took a deep breath. "You're probably right," he said. "But here we are. If you want to see the cairn, we'll show you. If not, we'll be heading back."

The man turned abruptly and stared out over the crater. He looked as though he was trying to think of something else nasty to say. He turned back. "Okay," he said, "show me."

He picked up his gear.

"By the way, what's your name?" my father asked.

The man paused as though deciding whether to tell. "What's yours?" he said.

"I told you when you arrived," Father said. "I'm Jack Mac-Donald. This is my daughter, Katie."

The man nodded. "Starkey," he said finally. "Ben Starkey."

"Okay," my father said, "let's go."

He turned and started walking back along the rim. Ben Starkey followed, his rifle in his hand. I followed Ben Starkey.

We hadn't walked far when I heard a faint grumble from

deep inside the earth. It stopped. Nobody else seemed to hear it.

Ten minutes later I heard it again, louder.

Ben Starkey stopped walking. "What's that?" he asked.

We all stopped.

"That's the volcano," my father said. "It does that sometimes. It's nothing."

"Don't sound like nothing to me," Starkey said.

The distant smoke was no longer a dark stream. It was rising in clouds. One cloud at a time, like smoke signals.

The rumbling grew louder, deeper.

Was the volcano angry?

It could kill us if it felt like it, I knew that. All it had to do was spew lava up into the sky, pour oceans of lava down its sides, kill everything in sight.

It had done that once.

"I don't like it," Starkey said.

"Not much we can do about it," Father said.

We started walking again. The rumbling increased, we felt a tremor, a second tremor, larger, noisier.

The shaking and the noise stopped abruptly.

You could almost hear the silence.

Starkey looked relieved.

When we came to the turnoff, my father headed downhill without a word. We passed through the trees and entered the clearing.

"There's the cairn," Father said.

Starkey walked halfway around it and put his pack down

on the far side. He came the rest of the way around to where we stood.

"Your son is not under there," my father said. "I guarantee it."

"That's what you say," Ben Starkey said.

"I can understand why you think differently," Father said. "So, Katie and I will help take the cairn down far enough so you can see for yourself. The three of us will take it down together, and after you're satisfied it's not your son, we will put it back up. Is that fair?"

Ben Starkey nodded assent.

"We're going to do this with respect for the man who's under there. That means you put both your guns down over there with your pack. We're not going to do this armed."

Ben Starkey stared at the cairn.

"Do we have a deal, Ben Starkey," my father asked, "or do we not?"

"We have a deal."

"Do you have gloves?"

"I have gloves," Starkey answered.

"Good," my father said. "We'll start by taking rocks off this end. We'll leave the other end alone as much as we can. After a while we'll come to a big, flat rock just over this person's head. Katie and I will lift that rock off, and you can have your look."

We all put on gloves. Father climbed on top of the cairn, took off the first rock, and handed it to me. I put it on the ground about ten feet back from the cairn.

"We'll keep the rocks in order as much as possible," he said. "Then we'll have a general idea of where they go when we put them back."

We worked steadily for an hour. My father handed rocks to me and to Ben Starkey, and we covered the ground in a sort of fan around the head of the cairn.

At the end of the hour Father said, "All right, Katie, let's switch places."

He climbed down off the cairn. I climbed up and started handing the rocks down.

At the end of the second hour we took a break.

We got our canteens. I drank slowly, sip, sip, sip, to make it last. We weren't really sure how long we'd be out here. Ben Starkey sat down on the grass and took a big gulp of water. He closed his canteen and lay flat on his back with his arms and legs spread out.

Ten minutes never seemed so short. Father timed it with his watch, but it still felt as though we'd just sat down.

My father climbed back up on the cairn and we started again.

"Ain't I got a turn?" Ben Starkey said.

"The person under here is our particular friend," Father said. "Katie and I built his cairn, and we feel responsible for how it gets taken down. Also, how it goes back up. No offense."

I don't think Ben Starkey minded. Balancing on the cairn and handing the rocks down was the hardest job, and we all knew it.

Late in the afternoon we came to the flat stone.

"Give me a hand, Katie," my father said.

I took hold of one side, he took the other.

"It's not going to be very pretty, Katie," he said quietly. "If I were you, I'd just lift. No need to look. Let Ben Starkey do the looking, then we'll set it back down."

I wasn't sure whether I'd look or not. I'd seen Dan Mills dead, and I'd helped bury him. Was that enough, or did respect require me to take another look, after the ants and maggots had done their work?

My father turned to Ben Starkey. "Go ahead. Take a look."

Starkey came over.

As we lifted the rock, I turned my head away.

"Is this your son, Ben Starkey?" Father asked.

Ben Starkey stood motionless, staring. He looked shaken. Finally, he shook his head.

"Say it," my father said, "yes or no."

His answer was a whisper. "No."

"All right, Katie. Let's lower it."

We put the rock back in place and started rebuilding the cairn right away. None of us said a word. We kept at it, stone after stone, till just before sundown. Then we ate, climbed into our bedrolls, and slept, Ben Starkey on his side of the cairn, we on ours.

TWENTY-FIVE

We finished rebuilding the cairn around noon the next day. We'd barely spoken since Ben Starkey had taken his look. He and I handed rocks to my father, who put them back in place.

After the final stone was in place, we picked up our gear, ready for the hike home. Ben Starkey strapped on his handgun, picked up his pack and his rifle.

Ben Starkey walked as though he was very tired. He slumped. His pack, his bedroll, his rifle weighed him down.

He was a disappointed man.

He hadn't done anything wrong. He hadn't attacked anyone. He was an innocent man who was trying to find his son, dead or alive. It seemed cruel not to tell him what had happened. It might be better for him to know the truth about his son than to know nothing, but we couldn't tell him. Ben Starkey would never believe us.

After an hour we took a rest. At this spot the trees grew close enough to the rim so we could rest in the shade.

"Mighty hot," my father said. It was the first thing he'd said to Ben Starkey since we'd uncovered Dan.

Starkey nodded. He looked uncomfortable. "I was wrong," he said.

Neither of us said anything.

"I was sure it was my boy."

"Well, now at least you know it's not," Father said.

"I thank you both," Starkey said.

My father nodded.

"You're welcome," I said.

My father looked at his watch. "Time to get going."

Lorraine was watching from the porch as we walked toward the cabin. She waved, and Father and I waved back.

Ben Starkey held back as we neared the porch. "I'll just ask for my horse," he said. "I've still got a fair amount of daylight. I might as well get started."

"We'll give you some more water," my father said.

"Thanks," Starkey said.

"How are you fixed for food?"

"I'm all right."

My father stepped onto the porch and gave Lorraine a kiss.

"Everything okay?" she asked.

"Fine," he answered. "We're going to give Mr. Starkey some water, then he wants to start back."

He turned to Ben Starkey. "Come on in, plenty of water."

"Thanks."

"I'll get your horse," I offered.

Lorraine came down the steps. "Come in, Mr. Starkey."

He seemed embarrassed. "I'll wait here till my horse comes up. I want to get my extra canteen out of my saddlebag."

"Have a seat while you wait," Lorraine said. "Katie will be back in no time."

Haltingly, Ben Starkey stepped onto the porch. He looked at the two benches, then at Lorraine, then sat down.

It didn't take long to saddle the mare and put on her saddlebags and the scabbard. Ben Starkey stood up as soon as he saw me leading her up the path.

He came over and put his rifle in his scabbard. He took a canteen from one of the saddlebags and another from his backpack and walked up to the porch.

"Right in here." Lorraine led him into the cabin and I followed.

My father stood by the water barrel, drinking from a pottery mug. He took the top off the barrel and picked up a dipper. "Give me your canteens."

"Smells mighty good in here," Ben Starkey said.

"I just made some bread," Lorraine said. "Here, sit at the table and I'll give you some."

"Don't want to trouble you," Starkey said.

"No trouble," Lorraine told him. "Sit down, I'll bring it."

Ben Starkey sat gingerly in one of the armchairs. He wasn't quite sure whether his pistol was going to fit inside the armrest or outside. He wriggled a little and made room for it inside.

Lorraine went into the cubby off the big room to get the bread. Father set the canteens down in front of Starkey.

I got the chair from my bedroom and sat down at the table. No one was speaking. It seemed very awkward.

Lorraine came back with four plates and a loaf of bread. "I'll cut you all some," she said.

As always, her bread was delicious. Ben Starkey ate his slice quickly, so Lorraine cut him another.

"I shouldn't," he said.

"Sure you should," she said.

Lorraine held out the slice of bread, but something else had caught Ben Starkey's eye—something in the shallow wooden bowl in the center of the table.

He reached in and picked up the silver magnifying glass. He ran his fingers over the front, then the back. He swung the glass out of its case on its swivel.

His whole manner changed. "Where'd you get this?" he demanded angrily. "Where'd you get this goddamn glass?"

"You recognize it?" my father said.

"I sure as hell do!" he shouted. "It belongs to my boy! How come you have it?"

Starkey stood up, pushed his chair back so hard it fell over. "I get it. It's all been a big show, ain't it!" His eyes widened. They moved rapidly from side to side. "All this business with that cairn, that was just a smoke screen, wasn't it! You show me my son ain't buried there, like you ain't killed him, when all the time you have killed him, and you've got him buried somewhere else!"

He walked toward my father, waving the magnifying glass in the air. "And here's the goddamn proof, my son's glass one of his friends give him! His glass with the silver case!"

"That is my wife's glass," Father said. "I bought it, I gave it to her when we lived back in New Pacifica. She brought it out here with her. Those are her initials."

"So now you're calling my boy a liar!" Ben Starkey thundered. "On top of everything else, you're saying it's her glass, and he's a liar, and you're all a bunch of angels!"

Fumbling with his holster, he pulled out his gun. "You're all in on it, ain't you! The whole rotten lot of you! Here, Mr. Starkey, have some water. Here, Mr. Starkey, have some bread! You wait, Mr. Starkey, I'll get your horse for you!"

His gun waved in the air. "Oh, you're a sweet bunch! Having your fun fooling poor dumb Mr. Starkey! Well, the fun's over!" He pointed the gun at my father. He swung and pointed it at Lorraine. Then he pointed it at me.

We pushed our chairs back, each wondering what to do.

"Put it down, Starkey," my father said calmly. "I've told you the truth about the glass. Your boy may have had one like it, but this particular one belonged to my wife."

"You took it off his dead body, didn't you!" Starkey yelled. "You not only killed him, you stole from him!"

"Put the gun back in your holster, Starkey," my father said.

"Let's sit down and talk about this like civilized human beings."

"Civilized? I'll give you civilized!" Ben Starkey screamed. He fired a shot into the ceiling. "Which one of you wants to get civilized first?" He fired again. "How's that for civilized?"

He pointed the gun at me. "How about you, girlie? You want to get civilized? Shall we show your old man what it's like when someone kills his kid!" He raised his other hand to steady the pistol.

I dove under the table.

I saw his legs. His head came into view, then the gun. He pointed it at me as I tried to scramble away.

Suddenly his body pitched sideways and tumbled, my father's body pressed hard against it. The gun fired, Ben Starkey fell to the floor, my father sprawled on top of him.

The gun fired again.

Ben Starkey rolled my father off him. Still holding the gun, he got to his feet.

My father lay on his back, motionless.

I screamed and crawled toward him.

Blood spread across his chest.

Lorraine knelt beside me. She took my father's face in her hands. Her hands were shaking. "Jack!" she pleaded. "Can you hear me, Jack?"

Ben Starkey stood over us. His eyes showed white all around his pupils. His mouth hung open.

He ran to the door. He stopped and looked at us all on the floor, still waving his gun.

I was in shock. I tried to scramble backward out of his view, knocked a chair over.

Ben Starkey looked stunned.

Then he ran out.

TWENTY-SIX

Lorraine pulled my father's hunting knife from his belt. She tore his jacket open, sliced through his shirt with the knife.

"Quick. Get me a clean cotton shirt, Katie," she said. "We need bandages. Then water."

I ran to Father's drawer, got a shirt, and gave it to Lorraine. I raced to get water.

Lorraine had my father's clothes off from the waist up. She felt for a pulse in his wrist, in his neck. She bent over, listened to his chest, put her cheek close to his mouth.

The blood oozed.

She put her head to his chest again, listened.

After a while I realized she wasn't listening anymore. She was weeping.

My father was dead.

I knew I should cry. I felt nothing.

My father had tackled Ben Starkey to save my life. He gave his life to save mine.

I felt numb.

Lorraine wept quietly, her head against my father's chest.

Ben Starkey had killed my father. My father was dead, he would never come back.

Ben Starkey was gone.

I stood up.

Unsteady, I went to the door, saw the upside-down box that covered our revolver. I lifted the box, saw the gun, put the box back. I picked up my quiver and my bow, ran out.

There was only one thing I could think of. Ben Starkey.

He was on horseback. That limited the ways he could get off the volcano.

Would he go back the way he came? It was the only route he knew. He would go north along the crater's edge. Somewhere short of The Crease he would start downhill.

He would go over. Then he would go down.

Two sides of a right triangle.

My father had taught me about triangles. About the hypotenuse, how to figure it.

I would take the longest of the three sides, but it would still be shorter than the sum of Starkey's two sides.

Horses were wonderful on open ground, not so good on the volcano. Too many rocks, boulders, stands of trees.

I was on foot and I knew the volcano. I could cross its

rocks and maneuver through its trees easily. My father had taught me how.

He had taught me many things. About triangles. How to move swiftly on the volcano.

How to hunt.

I angled quickly, silently downhill through the trees. My bow was strung. My arrows were at hand. I stopped, stood still, listened. Nothing.

I resumed my slanted path downward. I knew exactly where The Crease ended. It was marked on a map in my brain.

A cock pheasant whirred into the air. I barely looked.

As I neared the downhill end of The Crease, I saw a familiar landmark—a big rock covered with lichen with a twisted pine growing out of it.

To get around the bottom of The Crease, Ben Starkey had to pass that rock.

I looked for a rock of my own to crouch behind but couldn't find one. Instead, I found two bushes growing together, just high enough to conceal me, with a natural notch between them so I could watch.

Behind the shrubbery, I took out all my deer arrows and looked them over carefully. I picked the one that was straightest, best balanced, fletched with the newest feathers and fitted it to the string of my bow.

I kept scanning the uphill side of the volcano, listening.

I saw nothing, heard only the wind.

I was thirsty. In my haste I hadn't brought a canteen. Even

if I'd had one, I wouldn't have used it. One of the secrets of hunting, my father had told me, was to pick a good spot and stay still.

I thought I heard a noise.

I strained to listen. Nothing.

There it was again, a faint crackling of brush!

My heart beat faster.

A small rock tumbled. Had Ben Starkey's mare kicked it?

It came to a halt. All was silent.

Then I heard the sounds of hooves on rock. I strained to see through my notch in the bushes.

There! A flash of Ben Starkey.

Some trees hid him and his horse.

I saw more flashes. He was coming. Down the hill. Right toward me.

I tightened my grip on my bow.

He was leading his horse. It was too steep for riding. He was moving as fast as he could, but the terrain was rough. He slid over rocks and loose gravel. He was coming fast.

He was a hundred feet away. Seventy-five.

Fifty.

I stood up.

He saw me and slid to an unsteady stop. He dropped the reins and reached for his gun.

"You killed my father," I said.

I pulled my bow to full stretch.

His gun fired and a bullet whistled past me.

I let my arrow go.

It hit him just below his breastbone.

He jerked back. He looked surprised.

I had seen that look before.

Still facing me, he slumped to his knees.

His gun fired.

I felt a flame in my left arm.

Ben Starkey fell face forward into the dirt and stopped moving.

TWENTY-SEVEN

Warm blood trickled down my arm.

I dropped my bow, grabbed my arm. It was on fire, but it still worked.

The head of an arrow protruded from Ben Starkey's back. What had I done?

I took a deep breath, shook my head. I had no sensation inside me. I was still numb, the way I had been since Ben Starkey had killed my father. I had felt only a sense of mission, a task I had to perform.

Now I had other tasks.

I wriggled out of my buckskin jacket. The left arm of my shirt was covered with blood. With my good hand I yanked at my shirt buttons, squirmed, pulled, got the shirt off.

I could see where the bullet had hit.

I took out my hunting knife. Holding a sleeve in my teeth

and the body of the shirt between my knees, I somehow man-aged to cut both sleeves off the shirt. I folded the bloody sleeve into a small square and put it over the wound. I balanced this bandage on my injured arm and wrapped the clean sleeve around it. The bloody square didn't want to stay in place, but I finally got it so I could tighten the clean sleeve around it.

I tucked the sleeve end under the wrapped part, as far as it would go. It held.

Then I thought about what to do next.

My first thought was that my father would think I looked immodest, standing there with no shirt. Carefully, I pulled what was left of my shirt back on and walked over to Ben Starkey.

With my hunting knife I cut off the bloody arrow that stuck out of his back. I grabbed him with my good arm and tried to turn him over. He was heavy. It was too much for one arm, so I pulled with both arms.

The bandaged arm cried out, but I got him turned over.

The other half of my arrow stuck out just below his chest. I cut it off.

My father had said, "Never leave stuff around." I jammed both parts of the arrow into Starkey's jacket pocket.

The gun was still in his hand, so I laid it on a rock. I emp-tied the bullets from his belt and put the gun and the bullets in the pocket of my jacket.

I'd already decided what to do with the body, but I needed his rope to do it.

His little mare had been watching nervously, moving her

feet back and forth. I approached her slowly, talking softly. She jerked when I stroked her neck.

"There, there, baby," I said. "It's all right." After I stroked her for a little while, she began to settle down.

I took the coil of rope from her saddle. My plan was to drag the body, inch by inch if necessary, halfway up The Crease and roll it in.

I turned Starkey on his side. I wove the rope under and around his arms and tied them tightly. I tied his legs together separately.

I pulled on the knots. They would hold.

There was plenty of rope still left. I led it up the hill. I was now ready to start dragging Ben Starkey.

I doubled the rope around both hands, dug my heels into the hill, and pulled as hard as I could. Pulled, strained, used every muscle.

My wounded arm complained bitterly. Blood began to flow again under the bandage. I stopped pulling.

The body had moved about two inches.

I tightened the bandage on my arm.

I didn't want to bleed to death dragging him up the hill.

Ben Starkey's mare whinnied.

The mare! Of course! Let the mare do the work!

But how would I lift the body onto her back? Even if neither arm had been wounded, that was more than I could do.

Then it came to me. How could I have been so stupid? The mare didn't need to carry the body on her back, she could drag it.

My father's face flashed across my mind. I hadn't been thinking about him, and I knew I should. He was dead. Dead. The most important person to me in all the world was dead.

But all I could focus on was how best to hitch the mare to Ben Starkey.

"All right, baby," I said to the mare, "we're going to turn you around."

When I got her pointed uphill, I tied the rope to the saddle horn. I put my jacket and my bow and quiver on a nearby rock. It was familiar territory. I would get it all when I was finished.

I picked up the reins. "All right, girl," I said, "easy now, let's go."

The mare took up the slack in the rope.

"That's good, baby. Come on."

The mare felt around for footing, began to pull. Ben Starkey's body moved two feet. "Good baby," I said. "Once again."

The body moved nearly ten feet.

"Good, good, let's keep going." The ground was rough and the body jerked, but it kept moving. Fifteen feet, twenty-five feet, moving, moving. The mare wasn't at all happy, but she was doing a great job.

Starkey's belt caught on a snag, jerked the mare to a halt. The mare snorted and shook her head unhappily.

I unhooked the belt.

"Pull, pull."

The mare shook her head some more, then settled down and began to pull. The body moved. Farther, farther.

The belt snagged, the rope snapped, and the mare lurched forward. She jittered around nervously. I stroked her neck. "Stay calm, you're a good girl."

I managed to back her down a few feet. I tied the rope ends together with a sailor's knot my father had taught me. I knew it would hold.

"Here we go," I said, "easy now."

The body started moving again. He moved twenty feet, thirty feet.

The rope snapped again. The mare shied, almost bucked.

I wondered why Ben Starkey carried such light rope.

I knotted the rope once again, but the mare didn't like it at all now. She jerked at the rope, she shied at bushes, at rocks. Her eyes showed white all the way around the pupils. Ben Starkey's eyes had looked like that.

"Easy," I soothed, but she was through taking it easy.

She reared and pawed at me, reared again, and lunged. The rope broke. I lost the reins scrambling to get clear of her hooves.

Then she bolted.

She leapt over the body and started downhill at a wild, noisy clip. She skidded, lost her footing, found it again, side-stepped a tree, scraped another. The stirrups swung and the reins flew as she went out of sight.

Ben Starkey lay awkwardly in the middle of the path. Trussed up with his own rope.

At least my knots had held. The rope had parted in a new place each time. That was a grim satisfaction.

But the other end of that rope was going downhill fast, trailing behind the mare.

I looked down the hillside.

I saw a flicker of movement. Was the mare coming back? Unlikely.

I kept looking, listening.

Nothing.

TWENTY-EIGHT

My homemade bandage was completely bloody. I was in a pickle, and I knew it. I could never pull Ben Starkey up to The Crease all by myself.

Lorraine would help. And Billy. Lorraine, Billy, me, stronger rope. That was the answer.

Somewhere a twig snapped.

Uphill?

I looked uphill and saw no one.

I turned downhill. Nobody.

Then I saw him.

Almost hidden in the trees, about forty feet away.

Adam.

I felt a rush of pleasure. Then I felt panic.

The deputy sheriff.

The law.

Adam was holding my bow, my arrows, my deerskin jacket. "What's going on?" he asked.

"Adam," I said.

"What happened to your arm?"

I shook my head.

"I found your jacket and your bow," he said, coming toward me. "The jacket's all bloody. Here, let me see that." He looked at my arm.

"We've got to take care of that, Katie. Soon." He saw the body in the path. Bloody, tied with rope.

"What the . . . ?"

He scrambled down and looked. "My God, it's Mr. Starkey! What happened to him?"

"He's dead," I said.

"But how'd it happen?"

When the sheriff had come looking for Jess Starkey, he was already in The Crease. Now, his deputy had come looking for Jess's father. And there he was, lying dead in the middle of the path for all to see, the stump of an arrow sticking from his chest.

How could I explain that to the law?

Adam came back from the body. "Sit down," he said. "Let me take another look at that arm."

I sat on a rock. Adam lifted my arm gently and looked.

"We've got to get you back to your cabin," he said. "We've got to wash this, get a proper bandage on it."

I just looked at him.

"Do you want to tell me what's going on?"

I shook my head.

Adam was quiet for a moment. "Maybe you'll tell me later."

I nodded.

Adam offered a hand to help me up. "Can you walk? You can lean on me."

I looked toward Ben Starkey. "What about him?"

Adam glanced back at him.

"He's not going anywhere," he said.

"Let's deal with him now," I said.

Adam looked surprised. "What do you mean, deal with him?"

"Let's get it all over with," I said. "Is the sheriff around somewhere?"

"The sheriff?"

"He'll have to do a report," I said. "Like last time."

"The sheriff's not here," Adam said.

"You're doing the report?"

"Nobody's doing a report, Katie. I'm not here on business."

I stood up, holding my arm. I didn't understand.

"I quit the sheriff's department two weeks ago," he said.

My eyes widened.

"I'm here on my own business," Adam said.

"Your own business?" I said.

"I came to see you, Katie."

I couldn't speak.

"I promised, remember?" he said. "I said I'd come back. I've been thinking about you ever since I was up here, Katie. I wanted to see you again, see how you are."

I took a deep breath and looked up into Adam's deep brown eyes. My body came back to life a little.

We were both silent for a moment.

"I've got problems, Adam." I nodded down the path toward the body.

"What are you trying to do here, Katie?"

"Trying to drag Ben Starkey up to The Crease," I said.

"That big crack in the ground?" he said.

I nodded.

"I don't suppose you want to tell me why."

I shook my head.

Adam looked at Ben Starkey, then back at me. "I expect this is all for a very good reason."

I nodded again.

Adam was quiet for a few moments. "Well," he said finally, "how far do we have to drag him?"

My heart jumped. I pointed up the hillside. "See that big oak?"

Adam squinted. "Which one? That one way up there?"

"Yes."

Adam looked at the oak, then at the body. "Wow." He looked at the oak again. "That's a pretty good haul, isn't it."

"Can we do it?"

Adam made a wry face and groaned. "I guess we have to try."

"Oh, Adam!"

"It's just faintly possible," he said, "that if I do it in short stages, maybe I could carry him."

"He's too heavy!" I said.

"Maybe," Adam said. "Well, let's find out."

I felt so much better, now that Adam was here. The way he talked, the way he listened, the way he was ready to help.

He walked down the path and studied Ben Starkey's body. He cut the rope the mare had been dragging him with and stuffed it in Starkey's pocket. He pushed the body around until it was faceup, head pointed uphill.

Then he pulled Ben Starkey to a sitting position. He almost looked alive again. Adam crouched in front of him and folded Starkey's upper torso as far over his shoulder as he could. He worked his shoulder down until it was near Starkey's waist, put both hands on the ground, took a deep breath, and gave a mighty push.

He lifted, staggered, stood in a half crouch.

"Oh, Adam!" I said.

"It's a start," he grunted.

He took a step forward. He paused, made sure of his balance, and took another step. Another. Another.

He kept going until he had to rest. He put one knee on the ground, the body still over his shoulder.

"That's so hard, Adam," I said. "What can I do to make it easier?"

Adam didn't answer. He raised the body again, took a step, another step.

It took him about an hour to reach the big oak. Maybe longer. But he did it.

We stood at the edge of The Crease. The body lay on the ground a few feet away.

"This where you wanted?" Adam asked.

"Yes," I said.

He pointed to The Crease. "He goes in there?"

"He goes in there."

Adam pulled Ben Starkey's body around until it was parallel to The Crease, about a foot away. He stood up. He stretched his arms, stretched his back, his neck, his shoulders.

He looked at Ben Starkey, then at me. "You're sure this is what you want to do?" he asked.

"Very sure," I said.

"Really, really sure? Think about it."

"Really, really sure."

"Well, then," he said, "here goes."

He knelt behind the body, pushed, and rolled it over the edge. Ben Starkey disappeared without a sound.

Neither of us moved for a minute. Then Adam got wearily to his feet. We stood side by side, looking down the steep rock sides of The Crease.

I turned toward Adam.

He had trusted me.

He hadn't asked questions.

And he'd quit his job. He'd come back, just to see me. Just when I needed him most.

He looked at me questioningly.

"Ben Starkey killed my father," I said, and burst into uncontrollable tears.

TWENTY-NINE

I cried for a long time. Adam didn't say a word.

He put his arms around me and I pressed my face into his chest, crying, crying, crying.

Now I was all feelings. My father was gone. Dead. Gone forever. My father who I loved more than anyone in the world. My teacher. My protector. I didn't think I could live through pain like this.

I would never be the same. Nothing would ever be the same. The world would be gray, colorless. I would never hear his voice, his laugh, his gentle teasing.

Adam lifted my head. "Let's get you back and wash that arm."

My tears slowed, finally stopped. I took out my pocket cloth, wiped my eyes, blew my nose.

"I'm so sorry, Katie."

"Thanks." I reached over to pick up my jacket and my bow and arrows.

"I've got them, Katie," Adam said.

Lorraine was sitting on the porch when we rounded the north grove of trees. She got up and ran to meet us.

"You're bloody all over!" Lorraine said. "Good Lord, what happened?"

"I'm all right, Lorraine."

"Your arm," she said. "Let's get it cleaned up. You can tell me what happened while we're doing it."

"I want to see my father," I said.

"Of course you do, sweetheart," she said. "But right this minute your arm is more important. The sooner we deal with it, the better."

I hesitated.

"Your father would agree," Lorraine said.

She was right.

Lorraine turned to Adam. She seemed to be seeing him for the first time. "Deputy Summerfield."

"Not anymore, ma'am," Adam said.

Whether he was a deputy or not didn't seem to matter to Lorraine.

"Help me get Katie inside where I can work on her," she instructed.

We walked up to the porch.

"You sit here, Adam," Lorraine said. "I'll call you when we're through."

She sat me down at the table and untied the bloody sleeve that held my makeshift pad. She laid the sleeve on the table and started to lift the pad off.

I winced.

"Hurt a lot?" she asked.

"It's okay," I said.

"I'll take that for a yes," she said.

The folded-shirt bandage was stuck to my arm. My arm throbbed when she pulled it off.

"There," she said. She lifted my arm and looked at the wound closely. "That's from a bullet, isn't it."

I nodded.

She got soap, clean cloths, a bowl, a big pitcher of water. "This is going to hurt, but I've got to get it clean. That's the only thing to do with a wound like this."

"Okay." I knew it had to get clean.

Lorraine wet one of the cloths, soaped it, and began to wash my arm. She rubbed and rubbed, and the blood, which had pretty much stopped running, began to run again.

"Hold your arm up in the air," she said. "That'll slow the blood."

I held my arm up. She kept scrubbing the wound, rinsing it with clean water, washing, rinsing again with another clean, wet cloth.

"Ben Starkey?" she asked.

"I surprised him near the bottom of The Crease."

Lorraine kept on washing, rinsing.

"He shot at me twice," I told her. "The first one missed."

"Thank God!" Lorraine said.

"The second shot, I'm not sure he even knew what he was doing. He was falling. I'd already put an arrow in his chest."

Lorraine stopped washing. She took my head in her hands and pulled it to her shoulder. "Katie, Katie, Katie."

I thought about it. I had killed a man. I, Katie MacDonald, an otherwise nice enough person, had hunted another human being like an animal. I'd figured out his path, hidden, waited for him, surprised him, killed him. Put an arrow through him just like a deer.

Could I have let him walk away?

I didn't see how.

Living as we did, I'd come to respect all living things, especially the animals we killed for food. I would never kill one for any other reason, unless maybe a wolf or cougar, if it was trying to get at the horses or attacking me.

Had Ben Starkey been attacking me?

No.

But he'd killed my father.

My father! Tears began again.

Lorraine went back to washing my arm. She dried the wound with a clean cloth and inspected it.

"Another inch to the left," Lorraine said, "he would have missed you altogether. An inch or two the other way . . . let's not think about it."

"I was lucky."

"You make your luck. If your arrow hadn't gone home, who knows?" She stopped. "Where's Starkey now?"

"In The Crease," I said.

Lorraine raised her eyebrows.

"It was really Adam," I told her. "He carried him up there for me."

Lorraine re-bandaged my arm. "I'll get you a clean shirt."

I stood up and looked out toward the porch to see if Adam might be looking. He wasn't. I slipped the remains of the old shirt off and stood there, shirtless and bare, not a modest person at all. I looked at the back of Adam's head.

If he'd turned around and looked, I wouldn't have minded.

I almost called his name.

Lorraine came back with the clean shirt and slipped it on over the bandage.

"Adam," Lorraine called. "You can come in now."

I held my arm up. "Good as new."

Lorraine looked toward the bedroom where she and my father slept. "Shall we go to your father?"

"Yes."

"May I come?" Adam asked.

"Of course," I said.

My father was on his bed, lying very straight. He had on a pair of buckskin trousers Lorraine had made for him during the summer, moccasins, and his old deerskin jacket, the one he loved. His hair was neatly combed.

If his eyes hadn't been closed, you might have thought he was ready to go hunting.

The three of us stood there, looking at him.

My heart filled, I felt tears trying to come.

This is a mistake, I thought. This is not true. This cannot be happening. My father looked as though he were sleeping, taking a short afternoon nap after doing some heavy work in the morning.

"He has a suit, Katie," Lorraine said. "The one he wore the day we were married. Remember?"

"I remember," I said.

"I got it out and looked at it." She bit her lip. "It didn't seem right to bury him in a suit," Lorraine said. "It didn't seem like his kind of clothes." She turned to me. "What do you think?"

I could barely speak. "The buckskin is best," I said finally.

I couldn't take my eyes from him. My father, whom I loved, who had loved me, who had raised me, who had taught me so much. How could I live the rest of my life without him?

Surely he was asleep. He had been shot, like me. He had been bandaged by Lorraine, and now he was resting. In a while I would wake him. I would tell him about Adam coming back.

"We have to talk about where to bury him, sweetheart," Lorraine said.

Why couldn't he just stay there on the bed, and life go on as before?

That was silly, childish. My father was dead.

Dead like Ben Starkey.

Dead like Jess.

Dead like Old Dan Mills.

I thought about Dan, about building his cairn.

"We could build a cairn," I said.

Lorraine looked at my father, then at me. "I think he'd like that."

The thought of my father lying under a giant pile of rocks was suddenly too much for me. I threw myself on the bed and buried my head in his chest. Again I cried as though I would never stop.

Lorraine was crying, too. She knelt beside me and put her arms around me. I put mine around her.

"We both loved him so much," she said.

We held each other for a long time.

The next morning we picked a small, open field for the cairn, right next to the crater's edge. The field was south from the cabin, just around the first stand of trees.

We made this cairn differently from Dan's. First the three of us cleared and smoothed the ground. Then we covered a big, oval space with small, smooth stones, all about the same size.

We covered the stones with the tips of pine boughs. They smelled fresh and clean and made me think of everything that had defined my father.

We put his bedroll in the exact middle of the boughs, and we laid my father on top of that.

The three of us stood there, looking down at a sleeping man on a bedroll, in a sea of pine.

"I think now's probably the time to say something, Katie," Lorraine said. "I'd like to. I expect you would, too."

"I'm not sure what to say."

"Whatever you say will be just what your father would want," she said. "I'll start."

Lorraine knelt down and touched his cheek. She spoke slowly. "Farewell, Jack MacDonald. You are the kindest, sweetest, smartest man I ever knew, the best there ever could be. I loved you every day that I knew you. I'll love you forever."

Lorraine stayed kneeling for a minute. Then she kissed his cheek and stood up.

I still wasn't sure what I was going to say.

I knelt at my father's waist and sat back on my heels. I looked into his face. "Thank you for being my father." My throat tightened, and I thought for a moment maybe I wouldn't be able to go any farther.

I swallowed hard. "Thank you for taking care of me for so many years, Father. I realize now what a big job you had. Thank you for teaching me. Thank you for loving me. Thank you for saving my life. You've always known I love you better than anyone in the world."

I took two of the pine tips and put them in his hands. It was sad that on such a beautiful, warm day his hands should be so cold.

I bent over and kissed his cheek. I stood up, and Lorraine put her arm around me.

Adam cleared his throat. He stepped close to my father. "You were very nice to me, Mr. MacDonald, when I was here before. I appreciated that. It made me feel at home. I wish I'd had longer to get to know you. I know you were a fine man, Mr. MacDonald, and I'm sorry . . ."

He paused and looked at me, then at Lorraine. ". . . I'm very sorry you're dead."

Adam stood there a moment, as though he wanted to say more. Then he stepped back.

We put my father's favorite bow beside his right hand, his quiver of arrows near his left. When his body was covered with a blanket of pine tips, we started laying the stones, protecting his head the same way we had Dan's.

The largest stones went first. For each following layer we used stones that were slightly smaller. When it got dark, we went back to the cabin, ate a cold dinner, and went to bed.

At daybreak, we were back, building the cairn higher. It was mid-afternoon before we placed the final stones, four large ones in a row along the top.

They represented my father, my mother, Lorraine, and me.

As we finished, it started to snow. Another warning that winter would be here soon. But we weren't quite through yet. We picked up all the extra stones we'd brought to the site and carried them away, leaving the ground bare. Anyone who came to the clearing would see only the cairn.

THIRTY

Adam had slept on the porch the previous night. Lorraine and I had told him we had plenty of room inside, but he said he liked sleeping outside.

Our snow warning meant that was about to change.

"You can sleep in my room," I said. "I'll sleep with Lorraine." I'd already asked Lorraine. She'd said it was fine.

"I think I should sleep here in the big room," Adam said. "I'll put my bedroll near the fire and make sure it doesn't go out during the night."

"You don't have to worry about that, Adam," I said. "We always have embers in the morning. Besides, Lorraine and I are highly skilled fire builders. Aren't we?"

She nodded. "Highly skilled."

"Fortunately, I'm highly skilled, too," Adam said. "The

main thing is, I don't want to put you out of your room, Katie. And I like sleeping by the fire."

Lorraine looked at me and smiled. "I think Adam will be very comfortable in here."

It didn't snow again for three weeks, but Adam moved indoors anyway. It made me happy he was living with us, and it gave me a pleasant feeling of security that I'd never needed to think about before but was very glad to have now.

One night after Lorraine had gone to bed, and Adam and I were reading in front of the fire, I moved my chair next to his and said, "There's something you should know, Adam."

He looked mildly startled. "Sounds serious," he said.

"It is serious, but it's nothing we have to do anything about," I said. "It's just something you have to know. It has to do with the Starkeys."

"Ben Starkey?"

"His son," I said. "Jess."

"The one who got lost up here? The one the sheriff and I came up about?"

"He didn't get lost," I said.

Adam looked baffled. I stood up, walked over to the table, put my book down. I was stalling, I guess. I didn't like talking about this, yet I knew I had to. I went back and sat down.

"He got killed," I said. "The time I went to Badwater with my father, he picked a fight with me. It's a long story. I was supposed to be disguised as a boy and so on, it was my father's idea. Anyhow, he and I had a fight, and thanks to a trick Lorraine taught me, I won. He didn't like that."

"I'll bet!"

"So later on he came up the volcano. He wasn't looking for me especially, he was looking to steal some gold coins from my father. And he found me by accident. My father and I were out hunting together, but we'd picked different spots to hunt in. I'd just shot a big turkey, and it meant we could quit hunting and go back to the cabin, and I got careless. And suddenly I found myself face-to-face with Jess Starkey. Carrying a gun."

"That's awful, Katie!" Adam said. He turned his chair directly toward me so our knees were touching. "So what happened then?"

I took a deep breath, let it out. "I offered him my turkey, just in case he was hunting birds. I hoped he would take it and leave me alone, but I knew he wouldn't. He wasn't hunting birds, he was hunting our gold, and he'd found me, as a sort of bonus. He waved his gun around to scare me, he pointed it at me, and he made me hand over my bow and arrows. Then he attacked me, threw his big, ugly body at me, and knocked me down. He landed on top of me."

"Good Lord, Katie!" Adam said. He took my hands in his and pressed them together.

"He tied my hands to a tree and started to undress me. He was just opening his trousers when suddenly he sat bolt upright and gave a little cry. Then he started to fall, and I saw the tip of my father's arrow sticking out of his chest. And then he was dead."

I had started to cry. Adam knelt beside my chair, his arms around me. He held me tight.

"My poor Katie, Katie, Katie . . ."

I wiped my cheeks. I pressed my face against Adam's.

"I guess that's it," I said. "Except that Jess Starkey is in The Crease, same as his father. Lorraine and Father and I put him there. I had to tell you all this, because, well, it's part of me. And it always will be."

We sat in front of the fire, Adam holding me, for more than an hour. Neither of us said another word.

The weather turned fierce. Whenever it was snowing, Lorraine and Adam and I had to work hard pretty much around the clock to keep the snow from piling up against our door and sealing us in. We divided the night into three shifts. I took the first one, from nine to midnight. Then I would wake Adam up, and he would do the same thing until three. Then Lorraine would keep watch till six.

At six the three of us would clear the path from the cabin to the barn. We'd take care of the horses, and then we'd go back to the cabin and have breakfast. After breakfast one of us would clear a path to the cool house and chip the ice away from the spring. Whoever did that would bring back something good to eat—venison or some birds.

In between, there was lots of time to do whatever we wanted. We had the games my father had made—backgammon, checkers, and chess, including the elegant chessmen he'd carved. We also got out the old deck of cards Lorraine had brought from New Pacifica, and we taught Adam how to play poker.

Adam and I liked checkers and backgammon, but poker

was the most fun because all three of us could play. Lorraine had a big sack of polished pebbles, and each person got an equal number of pebbles to start out with. When you won a pot, you got all the pebbles that had been bet. It was a great feeling.

I read my old familiar books, over and over. Adam asked if he could read one, too. He said he'd never read much, but now was a good time to start. I gave him the book on King Arthur first. I thought he might like the adventure parts.

Adam liked that book, so I gave him *Frankenstein*, which he liked even better. Before the winter was over, he'd read every one of my books, plus both of Lorraine's.

I loved our games, but I couldn't help thinking about my father and how much he'd liked them, too. And I thought about how sad he must have felt after my mother died. He'd lived through a long winter during which she got sicker and sicker, every day a little farther from a chance of recovery. It must have been horrible to know she could die any day. Maybe today. Maybe tomorrow. Or, could a miracle happen?

I had never lived a single day thinking my father might die.

Part of me still expected him to walk in the front door, shake the snow off, and give Lorraine and me a kiss.

I knew Lorraine felt the same.

Once, the two of us were shoveling a path together out in the snow. Suddenly I looked at Lorraine, and we both burst into tears. We dropped our shovels and clutched each other. We didn't say a word. Then we got back to shoveling.

Sometimes, out of nowhere, I would begin thinking about Ben Starkey. He should never have done what he did. But he was looking for his son. It was terribly sad, a son and his father, both violent, both dead, both lodged in the hidden depths of The Crease.

Dead.

One by my father's hand.

One by mine.

I didn't like thinking about it, but I knew it would be with me forever.

Some nights Lorraine would say she was tired and go to bed early. She was letting Adam and me have a chance to talk, without anyone listening.

On one of these nights Adam said, "Are you going to live on the volcano forever, Katie?" Then he said, "I guess I asked you that once before."

We were sitting in front of the fire, staring at the burning logs. My chair squeaked as I turned it toward him.

"Where else would I live?" I said.

He turned his chair to face me. "Oh, I don't know." He thought a minute. "You said you wouldn't want to live in a town. And neither would I. I just wondered if . . ." He stopped. "I don't know what I'm talking about."

"I love living on the volcano," I said. "I can't imagine living anyplace nicer. Do you like it?"

"I think it's wonderful."

"Was it nice where you grew up?"

Adam stood up and stretched his arms over his head, then to the side. He leaned over and touched his toes. He sat down again.

"I liked the mountain I grew up on," he said. "It was nice. But I like this better. I like that crater."

"So do I," I said. "My father and I were going to hike all the way around it, but we had to cut it short."

"Maybe if I come next summer," Adam said, "we could do it together."

"What do you mean, come next summer?" I asked. "Are you going somewhere?"

"Not before the winter ends. But I can't just stay here forever, living in your cabin, eating your food."

"Well, it's your food, too. You help hunt it."

"I know," he said, "but it's your cabin. Yours and Lorraine's. I've got to think about building a cabin of my own."

"Why?" I asked.

Adam stood up. He picked up the blackened iron poker and stirred the fire. A shower of sparks flew up the chimney.

"Well, that's what my father did. Your father, too. It's sort of what men do to get started."

"Where are you going to build this cabin?" I asked.

"I haven't thought too much about it. Maybe even somewhere on this volcano."

"And are you going to live all alone?"

"Well," he said, "yes, till I get it built, I guess. I've pretty much got to. But then I'd like to do the same as our fathers did. You know, have a family. Something like that."

"Don't you need a woman for that?" I said.

Adam's face turned red. "Well, yes. Of course I do."

He went over to the water crock and dipped himself a drink.

When he came back to the fire, he said, "You know, Katie, I think I'll lay out my bedroll. I'm getting kind of sleepy."

As I climbed under my fur blanket, I found I was comparing Adam to my father. They were both very capable. Adam wasn't a carpenter like my father, but he was good at fixing things and willing to try anything. They were both strong. They were both honest. They were both the kind of people who would not give up easily.

I realized I was looking at Adam in a different light. Not just his brown eyes and his lashes, not the way he sat his horse, but what he would be like over time. As a husband.

I was a young woman, and he was a young man, and in some of my books that was the recipe for something romantic. I had even thought about Adam that way after seeing him in Badwater. But now it was different. We were different. And living in the world we did, it paid to be practical as well.

The next day, while Adam was clearing the paths and tending the horses, I sat down at the big table with Lorraine. She was mending a tear in her buckskin jacket.

"What do you think of Adam?" I asked.

Lorraine stopped sewing and lowered her hands onto the table. "I like him," she said.

"Is that all?"

"No," Lorraine said. "He's a very nice young man, and he's certainly a hard worker. You and I would have had our hands full trying to handle the snow and the horses and all without him."

"That's it?" I said. "He's nice and he's a good worker?"

"No," Lorraine said, smiling. "He's also very nice-looking. Have you noticed?"

I blushed. "Lorraine, you're teasing me."

"A little. Yes, I do like Adam. I like him a lot. From all I've seen, he's a very fine young man."

"I agree."

"He's dependable," she said, "and he's kind. That's a really important trait."

"He is very kind," I said.

"I think he has a good mind," Lorraine continued. "And he's strong. I don't mean muscles, although he's got plenty of those, but he's confident. He's strong in that way. He believes in his own abilities. He's not afraid of the world."

"He's strong and he's kind and he's gentle, and he's smart," I said. "I agree with all of that."

"Was there some reason you asked?" Lorraine said.

She smiled her kindly smile that said she was miles ahead of me in knowing what was on my mind. I got up, walked around the table, and sat down again.

"I want to ask him to marry me," I said. "What's your opinion on that?"

Lorraine put her jacket and needle aside and covered my hands with hers. "I think you two would make a wonderful couple."

We sat there quietly, not moving, for almost a minute.

"I do, too, Lorraine," I said.

"Are you sure you want to do the asking?"

"Why not?"

"The custom is that the man asks the woman," she said. "But customs change. Maybe that one has already changed. We're kind of cut off from custom up here."

"I know about the man asking," I said. "I'm just not sure he'll do it."

"Oh, I think he will," Lorraine assured me.

"But what if he doesn't?"

"Well, he's stuck here for the moment," she said, "so you can wait and see. The snow's going to be here awhile, and from what I see, he doesn't seem to mind."

I felt relieved and happy hearing her say these things. I thought Adam liked me, too, but sometimes I wondered if maybe it was all in my head.

"I think he likes you a lot," Lorraine said.

The winter wore on. Some snow melted, fresh snow came, the sun dipped in and out. On good days we led Billy and Valerie out from the barn and walked them up and down the paths to give them exercise.

A day later we would be snowed in all over again.

There came a day, though, when the sun came out, and it

seemed as though winter was ready to give up. That day, we all went outside and worked at our chores, and everything felt different.

The snow melted, and tiny streams of water ran everywhere. We didn't have to chip ice from the spring, and when we opened the barn doors, steam came out. We turned the horses loose to wander around the clearing in front of the cabin. For the first time in months, they seemed frisky.

By noon it was actually hot in the sun. The three of us brushed off the benches on the porch and sat down to enjoy the sun.

"I'm going to take a bath today," Lorraine said. "It's hot, and I'm tired of those little sponge baths we've taken all winter."

"I'll hitch Billy and bring up some extra water," Adam said.

"Don't bring any for me, Adam," Lorraine said. "I'm going to wash in the pond, cold as it is. Then I'm going to jump right out again and soap myself all over, including my hair, and then I'm going to jump back in and rinse. It's all going to take about thirty seconds."

"You're a brave woman, Lorraine," he said.

"Just a very dirty one," she replied. "Besides, when I'm through, I'm going to sit on that big, flat rock by the pond and get all hot and toasty again. How about it, Katie, you game?"

"Brrr," I said.

"It's not that bad," Lorraine said. "And think, we'll be clean!"

I stood up and walked to the edge of the porch. I took a couple of deep breaths. I stretched my arms over my head and turned around. "You sold me, Lorraine."

I looked at Adam. "How about you, Adam? You going to go jump in when we're all through?"

"Too high a price to pay for cleanliness," he said.

"You'll love it," Lorraine promised. "Think of it. You get clean, and you also get to splash around like a porpoise."

"What's a porpoise?" he asked.

"A big, happy fish," Lorraine answered.

"Then I guess I have no choice," Adam said.

There were still thin, flaky sheets of ice floating around the pond, but Lorraine and I gritted our teeth and jumped in. By the time we were through and sitting on the flat rock, letting the sun dry us, the shock of the icy water was entirely forgotten.

We felt wonderful. We put on clean shirts and underwear, and when we were dressed, we went back to the porch and told Adam the pool was all his. When he left, we sat down and combed each other's hair in the glorious sunshine.

A half hour later Adam showed up in a clean shirt, his wet hair combed, looking pleased with himself.

"You don't feel anything after that first jump," he said.

We sat there laughing and making jokes for more than an hour. The sun was hot on the porch. We were all very jolly, but a part of my heart was still cold and afraid. The coming of spring meant Adam might leave.

Why did Adam feel he had to build his own cabin? Because his father and my father had? It didn't make sense. Who said men had to do that?

That night Lorraine went to bed early.

Adam and I had spent lots of nights without Lorraine, but tonight was different. I felt excited and uneasy, both at the same time.

I wondered how Adam felt.

"Checkers?" I asked.

"Okay," he said.

I got the board and brought it to the table. We set up the men, but we didn't start playing. We just stared at the board.

Finally I sat up straight. I pushed the hair out of my face. "Adam," I said.

He looked up.

"I'm afraid you're leaving," I said.

I thought he'd look away, but he didn't.

"Before too long, I guess," he said.

"Going to build a cabin?"

"Can't stay here forever."

It was a strain, this intense eye contact.

"Are you ever going to get married?" I asked.

One of us had to look away now. But neither of us did.

"Katie, you know I don't have a place to take a wife," he said. "But I've got some money from working for the sheriff, and I'm going to buy some tools and stuff and get started."

"Got anyone in mind to marry?" I said.

At last Adam looked away. He stood up and walked over to the front window. It was completely black outside. After a minute he turned and came back. He sat down across from me.

"I want to marry you, Katie," he said. He paused, staring

straight into my eyes. "You know I've wanted to, ever since the sheriff and I came up here together. I thought about it even before that. Back in Badwater. I saw you, and something went off inside me."

My heart took a leap.

"I love you, Katie. It must stick out all over me," he said. "But how can I ask you to marry me if I don't have a home to take you to?"

I'd never seen him so serious before. Or so miserable.

"Don't sit way over there, Adam," I said. "Come over here and sit with me. Because, something went off inside me, too. I absolutely hated it when you left."

He came around the table and turned a chair to face me. He pulled it very close. "I hated it, too."

"Adam, whether you build a cabin now, or build one later, or never build one at all, I want to marry you, too. I love you, Adam."

"Really?" he said.

I looked straight into his beautiful brown eyes.

"Really, really, really," I said.

He put his arms around me. It was awkward, so I got up and sat in his lap. I felt jumpy and calm at the same time, and I liked the feeling. We sat there, not saying anything, then I laid my head on his shoulder, and he stroked my hair.

After a while he lifted my chin and kissed me, very gently. Then—and I liked this even better—not so gently.

We stopped. Adam's eyes were warmer, darker. He combed my hair with his fingers, lifted it off my neck, kissed me there.

I'd rehearsed some words all afternoon. Now it was time to say them.

I pulled my head away from him slightly. "I have the solution, Adam."

He brushed the hair away from the side of my face.

"I know what we should do," I said.

We looked into each other's eyes. Adam smiled.

"Tell me," he said.

"I have one question first," I said. "When we get married, we're going to be partners, aren't we?"

"Of course," he said.

"Partners all the way, right?"

Adam nodded. "Definitely."

"But you don't have a cabin yet. And that's what's keeping you from asking me to marry you, right?"

Adam nodded again.

"Well, I do have a cabin," I said. "And if we're going to be partners, only one of us has to have a cabin. Isn't that right? It doesn't matter which one."

Adam looked thoughtful. "It's not quite the same, Katie."

I put my face up close to his. I stared into his brown eyes.

"It's exactly the same, Adam. It's exactly the same. I'm dead serious."

He didn't say anything.

"Look at this cabin," I said. "It's just a bunch of logs my father dragged out of the forest. They didn't belong to anybody when my father came, and neither did the land. As of this moment it belongs to Lorraine and me. The day you and

I get married, it'll belong to Lorraine and me and you. It's that simple."

Adam was silent.

"It's just sitting here, crying out for us to use it," I said. "For you and me to use it, because we love each other and are going to be married, and for Lorraine to use it, because she belongs here. Except for you, Adam, Lorraine's my very best friend in the world."

Tears started down my cheeks. "Even if you'd just built an absolutely beautiful, brand-new cabin, it wouldn't be right for us to move into it. For one thing, we couldn't leave Lorraine. She needs us, and we need her. We all have a responsibility to each other. We all three need to live right here. You and I will be husband and wife and love each other and raise a family, and Lorraine will be part of it and be the grandmother, and we'll all help each other, and live here till we die."

I wondered if that was all too much for Adam. I couldn't quite read the expression on his face.

I'd said everything I wanted. Except for one more thing.

"So." I took a deep breath. "Will you marry me?"

His expression resolved into a smile.

He took my head in his hands. He tilted it back and looked in my eyes.

"Of course I will," he said.

THIRTY-ONE

Lorraine was delighted with our news. She turned into a different person.

She had a thousand plans. We should be married right away, not today, maybe tomorrow to give us time to get ready. Of course, it was all up to us, it was our wedding, but what was the point in waiting?

I should wear her green silk dress. Adam could be married in his buckskins. Or if he wanted, he could wear my father's suit and white shirt.

The big bedroom and the big bed would be ours.

We protested. No, she wouldn't hear of it. She would move into my room. She'd hoped this would happen. Adam was a fine young man, and I was her dear Katie-Bird. How pleased my father would be!

Did we want to be married on the edge of the volcano, the

way she and my father had? Or in the forest? What was she doing trying to run things anyway? she said. It was our business, not hers! She was just so happy!

I was happy, too, happier than I could ever remember. To love someone, and to be loved in return, was a beautiful gift.

"Lorraine," I said, "if it's all right with Adam, I want our ceremony to be exactly like yours. I want to say the same words you said. Can you remember what they were?"

"Heavens no," she exclaimed. "All I did was say what was in my heart. About how I loved your father and wanted always to take care of him. Just say whatever's in your heart, Katie. Whatever it is, it'll be perfect."

And so it came to pass. That's a phrase from one of my books. It came to pass that just before three o'clock on a beautiful spring day, Lorraine and Adam and I started putting on our best clothes to get ready for the ceremony.

Lorraine's green silk dress fitted me perfectly, but when I put it on, my rough underwear made lines in the fabric. I didn't want that. I wanted it smooth.

Lorraine said the same thing happened when she wore it.

"So what did you do?" I asked.

Lorraine gave a little shrug. "Who needs underwear?"

So I wore the dress the same way she did, and with my hair streaming down my back, as hers had.

The dress had bare arms. My arms were hardly ever bare. I looked at the scar on my left arm. I could see where the bullet had gone in and where it came out. The scar would always be there.

I didn't care.

When I finished dressing, I called Lorraine. "Would you help me with Dan's pearls, please?"

Adam wore his buckskins, but underneath his jacket he wore my father's white shirt. I was glad. It made me feel my father would somehow be present at the ceremony.

Lorraine wore white pants and a white shirt with a blue sash, her hair tied back with a white ribbon.

When we were all ready, we went out onto the porch. The air was clear, the sky filled with warm sunshine. The volcano smoked serenely.

"You both look beautiful," Lorraine said. "Yes, you too, Adam. You look beautiful."

"That's a first for me," he said, grinning.

"Well, shall we?" Lorraine asked.

Adam took my arm. We stepped off the porch and walked toward the edge of the crater.

Halfway there, Adam motioned us to stop.

He turned his head, listening. "I think it's a horse," he said.

We forgot the silk dress, the buckskins, the ceremony.

It was too far back to the cabin to get the gun in time.

Hooves on gravel. The squeak of a saddle. The horseman appeared around the trees to the north, his horse at a walk. He wore a gun belt and had a rifle in his scabbard.

I debated running for the trees.

"I can't believe it," Adam said.

"What?" I said.

"It's Sheriff Benson."

The sheriff rode up to us slowly and took his hat off.

"Afternoon, Mrs. MacDonald," he said. "Afternoon, Katie."

We both smiled and said hello.

"Hello, Summerfield," the sheriff said.

"Hello, Sheriff," Adam replied.

"Come to pay another visit?" Lorraine asked.

"I remembered how good your water tasted up here," the sheriff said. "Thought if I came back, you might give me another glass."

"Of course, Sheriff," Lorraine said. "Come on over to the cabin. We'll fill you up."

"But I'm interrupting something," Sheriff Benson said.

We started toward the porch.

"We'll tell you about it after you have your water," Lorraine said.

"I'll get it," I said.

Everyone was sitting down when I came back out. The sheriff's horse was standing in front of the porch, his reins trailing. I gave the sheriff his water.

"So what really brings you?" Lorraine asked.

The sheriff took a few swallows. He wiped his mouth on his sleeve. "It seems Badwater keeps losing citizens up here," he said. "They've asked me to investigate."

"How do they know this is where they lose them?" Lorraine said.

"Well," the sheriff said, "they've had an epidemic of horses coming back without riders. And when we check their tracks, turns out they've come from the volcano."

"An epidemic?" Lorraine said.

"Two," the sheriff said. "The last empty saddle turned up just before the first snows. Couldn't come while you were snowed in, but the family of the man whose horse it was asked me to come up and have a look as soon as I was able."

The sheriff took another swig of water. "I don't suppose any of you saw someone wandering around up here last October?"

"I did," Lorraine said.

The sheriff looked surprised. "That so?"

"A pudgy little man," Lorraine told him. "He came on horseback. He was looking for his son."

"That would be the man." The sheriff finished his glass of water and set the glass on the floor. "You'll remember when my former deputy and I came up earlier. We were looking for a young man. That's the son he was looking for."

"I remember," Lorraine said. "You and Adam."

"My deputy's left my employ since then. You may have noticed." He smiled at Adam. "If it doesn't swell your head too much, Summerfield, you're the best deputy I've had so far."

"Thanks, Sheriff," Adam said. "You were a great boss."

The sheriff went back to business. "Any of you know what happened to that man?"

"Yes," Lorraine said. "I know."

She turned to face the sheriff. "He thought his son was

buried under that cairn you saw last year. He said you hadn't done your job right, that you should have looked under it when you were here."

"He's told me that often enough," the sheriff said.

"He was very angry," Lorraine said.

"I know that, too." The sheriff stood up and took off his gun belt and put it under the bench. He sat down again.

"Jack didn't like him," Lorraine continued, "but he felt sorry for him. So he and Katie helped him take the cairn down far enough so he could see with his own eyes it wasn't his son. Then they put it back up."

"And the man?" Sheriff Benson asked.

"He came back to the cabin," Lorraine said. "We gave him some food and water, and then something sent him into a terrible temper."

Lorraine faltered. She took a deep breath and continued. "He was angry at all of us. He pulled his gun out and waved it all around. He fired a shot into the ceiling. He pointed the gun at each of us, then pointed it at Katie and asked if she wanted to go first. Jack rushed him, and he fired . . ."

Lorraine couldn't speak for a moment.

"He fired. Two shots. He killed my husband," she said quietly. "He killed Jack."

The sheriff shook his head, amazed.

"And that's what your missing citizen was doing up here on the volcano," Lorraine finished.

We were all quiet for a long time. Then the sheriff stood

up. "I can't tell you how very sorry I am, Mrs. MacDonald," he said. "I don't know what to say. I liked your husband. He was a true gentleman. That's a terrible, terrible thing you've told me."

Lorraine took a cloth from her pocket and wiped her eyes. "Thank you."

Sheriff Benson turned to me. "And you lost your father, Katie. I'm truly, truly sorry."

"Thanks," I said.

There was a pause when nobody said anything.

"Well," the sheriff said, "it sounds as though I'm looking for the right man, but for the wrong reason. He's not just a missing person now, he's a murderer."

"He is a murderer," Lorraine said.

"Well," the sheriff said, "with all you've been through, I hate to do it, but I guess you know I have to ask some questions."

"Of course, Sheriff." Lorraine nodded. "Ask whatever you need."

"Well, for starters, what made him so angry when he was in your cabin?"

"He thought the three of us were in some kind of conspiracy against him," Lorraine answered.

"Were you?"

"No."

"Then what made him feel that way?" the sheriff asked.

Lorraine shrugged. "He thought we'd tricked him somehow. He thought helping him with the cairn was part of the trick."

"How'd he get that idea?"

"I don't know," she said. "He seemed unbalanced."

"Hmm," the sheriff said. "So he got extremely angry, threatened you all, and ended up killing Mr. MacDonald. Then what did he do?"

"He ran out the door," I said.

"Anyone see where he went?" the sheriff asked.

"I was taking care of Jack," Lorraine said.

"I saw him," I said.

"Which way'd he go?"

"Around the trees on the north." I pointed. "The way you just came in."

"Anyone follow him?"

I had already thought about this question and how I would answer it. I tried not to hesitate.

"Around the trees? No," I said. "He took off lickety-split, and if I'd chased after him, he'd probably have shot at me."

Technically, that was the truth. I didn't follow him around the trees. But in my heart I knew I was lying. I didn't follow him around the trees, because I followed him a deadlier way.

"Hmm," the sheriff said. He folded his arms and sat quietly, his brow furrowed.

He mumbled quietly, frowning. "The horse comes back . . . dragging a rope . . . no rider."

He wasn't talking to us.

After a few moments the sheriff turned to me. "Nasty scar you got there, Katie."

I felt a shiver. I needed to answer quickly. "It's pretty well healed now."

Sheriff Benson was silent.

"Lorraine says it'll shrink in time," I said.

"What happened?" he asked.

"I got careless and ran into something."

The sheriff bent down and took a closer look. "Some something."

He turned to Adam. "You have any idea what happened to Mr. Starkey?"

Adam looked startled. "I wasn't even here, Sheriff."

"Hmm," the sheriff said.

Then he just sat.

And sat.

And sat.

Finally he broke his silence. "I hate to say this," he said, "because my job is to find this man, but I'm not sure I'm going to be able to do it. I'm going to keep looking, of course, but what with all the hazards of moving about on this volcano, I have a feeling I may never find him."

None of us said a word.

"He could have had some kind of accident," the sheriff said.

"That's a possibility, Sheriff," Adam said. "It's dangerous up here for a town man."

"His horse could have thrown him," the sheriff said. "He could have run into a bear."

Adam nodded.

"He could have . . . what do you call that big crack in the earth up north?" the sheriff asked.

"The Crease," Lorraine said.

"That's it, The Crease. God knows how, but it's even possible he could have fallen into The Crease."

"Any number of things could have happened," Adam said.

The sheriff cocked an eyebrow at Adam. Then he turned back to Lorraine and me. "Well, I'll keep looking."

I closed my eyes in relief. Then I opened them again quickly, in case the sheriff was looking at me. I felt like taking a few deep breaths, but I'd save that for later.

"One other thing," the sheriff said. "Probably of interest only to Summerfield. You remember that young man went hunting with his friend Jess Starkey? Came home early?"

"I sure do, Sheriff," Adam said.

"Well, he got himself a lot of money, God knows where, and first thing he got himself was a big, fancy pistol."

I froze. I knew just where he got the money!

"Only had it a week before he killed himself cleaning it," the sheriff said.

Nobody said a word.

The sheriff stood up. "You know, I didn't even ask why you people are all dressed up. You ladies look beautiful. Even Adam here doesn't look too bad."

Lorraine smiled. "We're about to have a wedding, Sheriff."

"A wedding," the sheriff said. "Well, I've been holding things up, and I apologize. You folks are all too polite to tell me. I certainly won't hold you up any longer. I'll be on my way, and you all can go ahead."

He stood and put his gun belt back on.

I liked Sheriff Benson. He'd said nice things about my father.

"No need to go, Sheriff," I said. "It's just Adam and me that are getting married."

"You and Adam," he said. "Well, my congratulations to you both."

"Why don't you stay?" I asked. "I've got Lorraine to be family for me. Maybe you could be family for Adam."

"Well, of course," the sheriff agreed. "I'd be proud to."

We all walked out toward the crater. I'd pretty well known what I wanted to say to Adam before the sheriff came, and now I began trying to bring it back to mind.

As we reached the edge, I looked out over the volcano. Huge clouds of smoke were billowing high into the air. Adam and I faced each other.

I felt a slight tremor. Adam felt it, too. We exchanged a glance.

From deep within the earth came a low grumbling. It grew louder, growling, primitive, relentless.

Another tremor came, stronger. Everyone felt it. Then the earth began to shake in earnest. The growl turned into a series of muffled booms.

The shaking grew more violent. Tall pines waved back and

forth. A pile of rocks at the edge of our clearing shook, tumbled, and fell into the crater. Our cabin swayed, shifted. The front door swung inward, swung back out, slammed, swung inward again.

The booming grew louder. The ground bucked and heaved.

I could barely stand. Adam grabbed me, and we helped each other stay upright. The sheriff took Lorraine's arms and steadied her.

How long had it gone on? A minute? Two? It seemed like hours.

The booming stopped.

The shaking slowed.

At the edge of the trees I saw the sheriff's horse, white-eyed, terrified, his reins trailing.

"The horses!" I shouted.

Adam raced toward the barn. The ground was still having small spasms. I hitched Lorraine's long silky gown up over my knees and took off after him.

Running down the path, I saw that the shed at the back of the barn had fallen.

Inside the barn, both horses were wild with fear. Adam had already put a rope hackamore over Billy's head and was doing the same with Valerie. He handed me Billy's rope, and I led him, kicking, shying, out into the sunshine. Adam followed with Valerie. We led them up the path to the cabin.

The shaking had stopped now. The sheriff was telling his horse everything was all right.

Everything looked just as it had before the earthquake. Placid. Calm. Beautiful. Smoke from the volcano was still heavy, but it was steady. The pines stood erect, their boughs moving gently in the breeze. The cabin looked as if nothing had happened. The horses, now reassured, were standing idly in front of the cabin, watching us.

Adam and I went into the cabin, and the sheriff followed. Lorraine was already there. She came toward me, put her arms around me.

"Are you all right?" she said. "I can't believe this happened."

We looked around the cabin. Chairs were tipped over and shelves had emptied onto the floor. Cooking pans lay here and there.

The eagle my father had carved for me was lying in front of the fireplace.

I picked it up. It was unhurt. I held it in my arms. My dear, dear father. I would go soon and see how his cairn had survived.

"We've been lucky," Lorraine said. "I don't see any major damage. A few things spilled, that's all."

"And we're all safe," the sheriff said. "Horses, too. That's about as lucky as you can get."

We started picking up the cooking pots and putting things back. Adam and the sheriff righted the chairs and put the furniture back where it had been. It wasn't long before the big room looked more or less like its old self.

For a moment we all stood there, looking around, not speaking.

"Well," the sheriff said finally, "seems to me we have some unfinished business to attend to."

So, once again the four of us walked out to the edge of the crater. As Adam and I faced each other, I could see Valerie and Billy and the sheriff's horse cropping grass contentedly.

The sun shone, the volcano smoked, and this time the earth held perfectly still. I got to tell Adam the same kinds of things Lorraine had told my father. About how I loved him and never wanted to be separated from him. Adam said the same sorts of things to me, but in his own wonderful words.

The sheriff pronounced us husband and wife.

And so we were married.

Lorraine kissed us both. The sheriff congratulated us.

"Well, it's time for a wedding supper," Lorraine said. "What do you say?"

"Do you really want to do that, Lorraine?" I asked. "After that earthquake and all?"

"Of course I do," she insisted. "Just give me a little time to get things going."

"I'll help," I said.

"No, no, this dinner is all mine," she said. "You go sit on the porch and act like a dignified married lady."

"Let me help," Adam said. "What can I do, Lorraine?"

"You can get a fire going, Adam," she said.

"Your dinner sounds wonderful, Mrs. MacDonald," Sheriff Benson said, "but God knows what's happened down in Badwater. I'd better hightail it back there."

He turned to Adam and me. "Before I go, however, I want

to say something to Mrs. Summerfield, and to you too, Adam. I wish you both the longest and happiest of lives. I truly do."

I was Mrs. Summerfield! I loved the sound of that!

Adam shook hands with the sheriff, and I threw my arms around him and kissed his cheek.

THIRTY-TWO

While Lorraine cooked a leisurely wedding dinner, Adam and I walked along to the edge of the crater until we came to the field with my father's cairn. Grass had grown all across the field we had so carefully cleared of stones, and it all looked very serene.

Miraculously, the earthquake had left it almost untouched. A few stones had tumbled down, and Adam put them back where they belonged. We walked to the side of the cairn and faced the head.

"I married Adam this afternoon, Father," I said. "In front of the cabin, the same place you and Lorraine did."

I looked out over the crater, then back at the cairn. "But you know that already. You were there.

"We're both immensely happy," I said. "And I want to tell

you not to worry about Lorraine, Father. We're all going to live in the cabin together, and take care of each other."

Adam cleared his throat. "I love your daughter very much, Mr. MacDonald, and I'll always take care of her. I want you to know you can count on that."

We stood there silently for a while longer.

"I'll always miss you, Father," I said, "and I'll always think about you."

When we got back to the cabin, we found that Lorraine had somehow managed to shift everything between the bedrooms. Adam and I now had the bedroom she and my father used to share, and she had mine.

It was a glorious venison dinner. We sat around in our best clothes and ate and ate, and talked and talked. We talked about the ceremony, about the earthquake, about how lucky we all were.

I found myself thinking about the sheriff's visit. "I wonder what Sheriff Benson really thinks happened to Ben Starkey," I said.

"He doesn't just think," Adam said. "He knows."

"What do you mean?"

"He's got it all figured out," he said. "He's the smartest man I ever met. He knows what happened to Mr. Starkey down to the last detail. He knows how he died, he knows where the body is, and he knows I helped."

"He doesn't care that I killed him?"

"There's an old judge down in Badwater," Adam said. "He holds court, he tries cases, and he thinks he's the law. But the sheriff is the real law. He's the one decides who's done right or wrong."

"And he punishes the wrongdoers?" I asked.

"No, the judge does that. But nobody makes it into court unless the sheriff decides to bring them."

"How do you know that?"

"I worked with him for two years. I know how he thinks."

I shook my head in wonder.

Before Lorraine went to bed that night, she gave Adam a kiss on the cheek. "I'm really glad you and Katie are married, Adam. I'm glad we're all going to be living together. I feel very lucky to have you and Katie as my friends."

She turned to me. "I'm proud of the woman you've become, Katie. Your father would be so proud. I wish he were here tonight. We both wish that, of course."

I put my arms around her.

"But I have another wish," she said. "I wish you were my very own daughter."

I closed my arms tight around her. "I am, Lorraine."

Adam and I sat by the fire awhile after Lorraine left. It didn't take us long, however, to realize we didn't want to sit by the fire. We wanted to go to bed.

"I'll shut the door," I said.

Before I shut it, I took a look out over the blackness of the volcano.

"Come look, Adam."

We stepped out onto the porch.

Miles away in the middle of the volcano, fiery red lava spouted into the air, higher than I'd ever seen. A red stream shot up, hesitated, fell back, and was replaced by two new streams. It was brilliant, the only light in the dark sky.

"It's putting on a little show for us," I said.

Adam put his arm around my waist. "It's happy for us," he said.

I went into our new bedroom first, and Adam followed. He closed the door, and when I turned around, he was standing right behind me. He put his arms around me and we just stood there, smiling at each other.

"I guess we're going to sleep together," I said.

"I guess so," he said.

I kicked off my moccasins.

"I guess we'd better take our clothes off," I said.

"I guess we'd better," he said.

He didn't let go, though, so I kissed him, and he kissed me back, and we just stood there for a while, his mouth on mine.

Finally I said, "I've got to get out of Lorraine's dress. Would you help with the buttons?"

I turned my back and lifted my hair so he could see. One by one he undid the buttons, taking his time and brushing my hair with his face.

"You smell good," he said.

When the last button was undone, I turned to face him. I

hesitated a moment, then slipped my shoulder straps off and let the dress fall to the floor.

Now it was just me, and Old Dan's pearls.

For a moment Adam looked stunned. Then he pulled me toward him.

His jacket buttons pressed against my skin. His belt buckle felt cold.

After a while I said, "Your turn."

Adam stepped back and kicked off his boots. He stood still as I took off his buckskin jacket.

"Adam Summerfield," I said. "Adam. Summer. Field. I love your name."

I undid his shirt buttons and slipped my hands underneath. He was smooth and warm. I pulled his shirttails out of his pants. I helped him get his arms out of the sleeves.

I undid his belt buckle.

"You take it from here," I said.

It was strange being in bed with a man. I had thought a lot about Adam. I had thought about his good looks, and about how I liked being with him, and about wanting to marry him, and spend my life with him, and have a family with him. I wondered now why I hadn't spent time thinking about being in bed with him.

Adam put his arms around me, and I put mine around him. There was barely enough light to see his face. He kissed me. I kissed him back. It was all very strange and exciting, and very, very warm.

Somewhere in the middle of the night I woke up. It was

too dark to see anything, but I could feel Adam close beside me, making me feel secure.

As I stared up into the darkness, I thought about the day I'd had.

Our first try at a wedding was interrupted by the sheriff. Our second try was cut short by the earthquake. Our third try worked beautifully, just the way I'd wanted. Then came our visit to my father, and Lorraine's venison dinner. And the volcano's fiery show. And finally, Adam and me, the two of us, in bed together.

It was some kind of miracle.

I thought about my trip to Badwater. On the fifth day after my sixteenth birthday. What a child I had been! I thought I knew everything. I knew how to ride and hunt birds and skin out a deer, but in reality I was an innocent.

I had wanted to see people, see the world.

I had seen quite a bit since then.

And now, nine days before my seventeenth birthday, I was lying in bed with the man I would spend the rest of my life with.

I thought about my life so far.

I'd been attacked by a man. My father had saved me.

I'd been attacked by another man. My father had saved me again. At the cost of his life.

I'd killed a man.

I stopped and thought about that for a minute. I'd killed a man.

And I'd lied to the sheriff about it.

Killing was a serious, serious thing. And lying was a serious thing. My father had taught me that. I knew I should feel guilty.

I wondered why I didn't.

I was sorry about Ben Starkey, truly sorry.

I thought about what Adam had said. There was a judge in Badwater, but in his part of the world the sheriff was the law.

Maybe in my part of the world I had to be the law. Maybe that was the way it worked. And maybe Adam and Lorraine had to be the law, too.

Lorraine and my father had loved each other dearly. I had Adam now, but what did Lorraine have? She had me and Adam, but what were we compared to Jack MacDonald?

We would always love Lorraine. We would always help her, she would help us, we would always be family.

Adam stirred. Adam, my special, special love. Mine, all mine, my very own. Closer to me than anyone else in the world.

I wondered if he was awake.

He put his arm around me and kissed my ear.

Adam. So sweet. So warm.

I snuggled closer.

About the Author

James Nelson has been a magazine editor in New York, a starving freelancer in rural Sonoma, a creative director for a San Francisco advertising agency, and the author of four non-fiction books. *On the Volcano* is his first novel. James's inspiration for this book began with the idea of a girl in her teens describing the lonely and solitary place in which she lives—an enormous, unexplored crater. He then assembled a unique setting from spare parts of volcanoes he had seen or read about, coupled with chunks of the Rocky Mountains he grew up next to. James Nelson lives with his wife, Mary-Armour, in Marin County, California.